VOICE & VEIN

A BROADSIDES NOVEL

MAKARI CLOVE, PUR DURANCE

AURICHALCUM PUBLISHING

• • • ●•• ● • • •

Trigger warnings: Assault; killing.

Content warnings: Graphic descriptions of organs; manipulation of blood outside
the body; injuries to eyes; instances of physiological body horror; forced memory-loss;
magical coercion.

CONTENTS

ONE

THEFT FROM A MORGUE

"You lost the corpse," Kian repeats with precise amounts of disdain and disbelief. This is not something the coroner appreciates: she gives him an indecently flat look in return.

"Look, don't look at me," she says. "He came in as an unidentified homeless person, and sometimes unclaimed bodies need to be cleared out. Do you know how much space we use down here?"

"A crypt's worth, I'm sure," answers Kian with great asperity. "You said he was autopsied. Did you at least remove the organs? Virchow or Letulle?"

The look the coroner gives him now is slowly flavoured with consideration, the sort of look with which Kian's quite familiar and supposes she isn't. Working in a morgue is not customarily considered sexy, unless one also works in a morgue. "Virchow," she says. Damn. That'll make a reanimation more difficult. "Why?"

1

"I need them," Kian says simply, and gives her his most charming smile, and within half an hour he's walking out of the morgue with a canvas cool-bag full of organs in formalin, and a dinner-date for the weekend for which he may even show up. He tries not to ruin potential professional relationships. ... Often.

The frustration here is that there's nowhere in the immediate vicinity where he can stow the bags and rescue the organs from the formalin; and even if there was, they'd be unlikely to stand up for themselves. No, he needs a place he can take his time — somewhere which preferably doesn't involve a coroner who thinks she's getting lucky. Unfortunately, it's also two in the morning, and he hadn't come out prepared to break into some poor schmuck's office to set up something he'd have to clean up later, or be satisfied with the aforementioned poor schmuck being arrested for an apparent crime-scene if he didn't.

Which means he may as well just head straight back to the church; joy of joys. Kian's too dignified to sigh, and thus he doesn't; but he'd really like to know what the senior clerics were thinking when they sent *him* to London, because surely it didn't involve being cajoled into performing basic errands an acolyte, frankly, could do.

Or maybe it did. The church as a whole has grown ever more insular in the last century, and he's gained a reputation for being willing to work outside its walls.

Kian does not move too fast, nor too slow; he's keenly aware of the fact that he's a well-dressed man in Tower Hamlets, right down to the cane, and Canary Wharf is far too far to be of any benefit except to tower brightly as a reminder of what well-dressed peoples typically possess. It's funny how many landmarks wound up in the poor side of the inner city. He heads towards Tower Hill, which is a *fantastically* cliché place for the church to want to reside in London. Unluckily for them modern administrations are a little too good at keeping out the riffraff, or at least riffraff in large numbers, so the church has had to settle for a place close-by in Whitechapel, near the railroad.

He passes unobserved through the borough up until he's a few streets from the Hill, close enough to feel the warmth of it in a relative distance, like a fire on a horizon. The church is on the other side: he has the opportunity to stroll up Tower Hill Road straight through the area, which is rather like ambling between the sun on one side and warm reassuring stone on the other — for certain types of people, anyway. It's a walk he's done before since arriving in London. This time before he really reaches the Tower, at a place on the road where buildings fall away to his right in favour of concrete blocks and a square, a jogger passing in the other direction brushes by; and really the only reason Kian doesn't wind up with a blade between his ribs is that the jogger feels far too cold to be non-magical.

Instead ice splinters against canvas as he raises the bag just enough to deflect, and both cold and shards make his hand sting. They both turn in the same moment and Kian's cane wins; the air is filled with the sharp smack of timber on flesh and the jogger grunts and drops the shard in their other hand. That's a novel means of assassination, to be sure.

If it is an assassination, Kian realises a little too late to stop the jogger from grabbing the bag. Bloody hell, if they'd wanted the organs they should have stolen the body *before* it was autopsied!

Kian grips the bag tighter and keeps walking. Either the jogger will have to let go and keep on going, or turn and declare violent intentions directly, where there may even still be *someone* nearby to see it. They're just down the road from the Tower of London, for God's sake. The jogger chooses to declare: Kian hears the tell-tale step and radiating cold, and in a neat hop-and-step he avoids the slash of an icy blade toward his back, his coat whirling elegantly behind. He's expecting maybe a dagger in the arms of a hooded assailant; instead he gets a bloody great *sword* reverse-slashing toward him, and skips back another step, on top of one of the concrete blocks splitting square from street.

Running's undignified, but Kian casts dignity to the night and takes off toward the path leading to the Tower proper using the concrete blocks, stepping easily over gaps. Using magic in public — honestly.

The jogger's faster: they hurdle one behind and come up on his right to slash at his feet, forcing him away from the square and the path. Kian could've managed that by making a break for the Tower Hill Memorial instead, but just as he angles to dash across the road a car comes roaring out of Trinity Square, absolutely ignoring lanes to rush him across potential oncoming traffic.

Cursing Kian turns and yanks on the death behind him, just close enough with its power to respond and save him from taxing himself; the car slams into him and the shield of shadow absorbs the blow down to merely rattling. Not enough to stop him from being flung backward into the iron fence or feel it buckle under his weight and the car's kinetic force; he tumbles backwards into the garden and something rebounds off a tree straight into his leg. Screaming, at this point, is an unfortunate — or perhaps fortunate — reality.

"Hey!"

The car pulls away from the kerb and the fence with an unholy screech of wrought-iron on steel, and Kian hears a door slam. Running footsteps segue with his roaring pulse. Kian pulls the bag closer and reaches out again, this time for shadows across the way. Being pulled through them from one place to another is usually like stepping through a warmly lit door: on this occasion it feels more like being thrown into a roaring furnace. He comes out somewhere on Trinity Square flushed and shivering, and almost at once buckling to the ground with some*thing* in his leg.

Something, he notes distantly, which is thankfully not an ice shard of some kind: just a remnant of the fence, which has been misplaced through his thigh. He takes some deep, slow breaths, resisting the urge to yank the damn thing out; it takes some time before hot nausea and dizziness recede enough to act.

Damn it all. Now he's going to have to get a new pair of trousers tailored for this suit.

And a new tie. His hands tremble as he reaches up to yank this one undone, shifting as little as possible as he winds that around his leg and pulls it taut on either side of the bar. That still doesn't stop him from needing to bite on his label in lieu of airing his position to whoever else might be angling to drive cars into innocent bystanders such as himself.

If the church had bloody well known this was a possibility and neglected to tell him, he's going to wind up saying something very unwise to a superior cleric.

He sits for some moments more after that, gulping down air and figuring out where on Trinity Square he is. The church isn't far — but the assailants would surely be expecting him to go there. If he recalls from his amblings and his research since he arrived, there's a healer's clinic that's closer, a few blocks northward on Lloyd's Avenue. It's the kind of place with which the church wouldn't bother, if it remained sufficiently small, no matter how close.

Kian gives himself precisely ten seconds more and then scoops up the bag and levers himself painfully to his feet with his cane, gritting his teeth against any further urges to scream. His leg throbs and the blood oozes toward his shoe, which is just lovely; but the worst thing is when he hefts the bag and realises some of the organ jars have smashed and now there's formalin dripping from the canvas and into his *other* shoe.

Wonderful. Truly delightful.

May they be a load for four before the year is out — and Kian would be pleased to help them on their way.

With a deep breath Kian proceeds northward, leaning heavily on his cane and only lightly on that foot. He still feels as if someone's grinding a hot nail into his thigh with every movement. Lloyd's Ave is almost a straight shot up Cooper's Row, and at this time of night no one's going to bother with a man limping around with support. Kian keeps a close eye out and keeps to the shadows save when he has to cross the road, and doesn't dare stop moving until he reaches the place the little clinic had been.

There's stairs. Of course there are. Kian keeps a good grip on cane, bag and fence, and eases himself down one step at a time; and when he gets to the little lamp-lit landing at the bottom, overshadowed by building and by road, he feels like death warmed over. This is not all that much of a euphemism, in his circle.

He rallies enough so as to *not* fall into the room immediately upon opening the door. There's the little jingle of a bell, how charming, and across the room a woman with faintly luminescent white hair. The luminescence isn't all that encouraging, being indicative of either someone non-human or a light-aligned, but the dying can't be choosers; and especially not given the weave on the wall declares a more-than-passing familiarity with traumatic-injury reconstruction, which is not precisely common in tiny clinics like these and could well be his saving grace if his leg is as lacking in blood circulation as it currently feels.

Kian leans against the jamb, bleeds on her floor, and gives her his most charming smile under the circumstances. "Ah, Healer. May I beg your indulgence for some assistance, if you please?"

TWO

STRANGERS BEARING ORGANS

M ore than once Rosemary has considered keeping less odd hours; and just as often she's discarded the notion. It isn't as though she's hard to rouse in a genuine emergency, and most of her clientele appreciates that she's available to see them in evenings, outside of standard work hours or sunlight or well-trafficked roads.

The idea of sleeping at regular hours sometimes comes back to her at times like these: three am and change, tidying files as she waits the extra half-hour just to see if her last no-show is going to turn up late. The files could do with the ordering, anyway — she isn't so profitable or busy that it's necessary to hire any kind of assistant, but as a consequence if things don't get done she has only herself to blame. She hesitates over the file for today's no-show when she comes to it. Reed, transplant follow-up. Her water alignment seems to be helping the adaptation, even if her discipline is in plant magic. All told, the rejection risks here are much lower than they would be in the average person, but she's still going to be seeing Ms Reed every other week or so for the next several months, until the genetic assimilation is complete.

She flips the file closed, stretches back in the chair. Her back cracks, aches in a way that suggests she's been sitting bent over at least an hour too long, and a yawn takes over. Well. Give it another twenty minutes, and she'll consider that due diligence has been done, and follow up with Ms Reed tomorrow.

The bell over her door rings as she straightens up again. Rosemary assumes at first it's the much-delayed Ms Reed, and looks over with a greeting on her lips —

The splatter of dripping liquid and accompanying scent of blood, and a much taller figure than she expected. Not her predicted patient, but certainly someone in need of help. He leans in the doorway, a long streak of darkness with a smile that is probably intended to be charming, and even might be if Rosemary wasn't so focused on the actual problem. She can tell even from here there's metal through his thigh, though not the precise sort. It doesn't matter immediately.

"Ah, Healer. May I beg your indulgence for some assistance, if you please?"

She's already on her feet and moving toward him, file temporarily forgotten. Magical presence — yes, something warm she doesn't have time or focus to further examine right now. "Lean on me," Rosemary instructs, slipping up beside him. "Don't put any more weight on that leg if you can help it."

It's not an administrative assistant she should hire, it's a nurse with exceptional muscles. Honestly.

His hands are full, a cane in one, a dripping bag in the other. Cane is good support — she cycles through possibilities of old injuries and limps before discarding them in favour of the fresh injury. The bag doesn't make much sense, but when Rosemary tugs to take it from him she discovers his grip strength is still good, and that he doesn't want to let go of it.

"Fine," she mutters. It's not worth the effort if he has good enough hold of it. The sharp scent of it is resurrecting memories of med school, preservatives and study of old, long-kept parts of the human body, and when it moves it chimes in the way of glass against glass. "This way —"

She gets an arm around his waist and between them they shift his weight toward her. The injured stranger has at least a head on her, if not more, so he has to lean partially down instead of over, but Rosemary is steady enough. Even if flinging him over her shoulder is out of the question for now.

"Operating room is this way," she says briskly. His hand is a little cool to the touch, which could be indicative of shock or could reflect a magic that results in lower average body temperatures. Right now, it's just data to be filed.

The space between the front door and the bare room she has set up for treatment has never seemed quite so long. The stranger's steps drag with an uneven counterpoint of sounds, the thump of cane against the scrape of his bad leg, and there's blood in their wake. Clean later; healing now. "Sit," Rosemary says, gesturing at the metal table. "Do you need assistance?"

"A moment." He leans more than sits, pitching toward the metal surface. His hands are too full to catch himself, so it's Rosemary that steadies him. "Ah. Perhaps."

Rosemary will take 'perhaps' as 'yes, please.' She knows the sort. "All right," she says, and helps him get situated, bearing the weight of the injured leg up so he won't need to strain the muscles. He manages the cane with the absent ease of someone used to accounting for it, tucking it against his side. "Will you give me that now?" At his visible hesitation, she adds, "It won't leave the room."

He studies her a moment longer, dark eyes sharp despite clear pain and blood loss. "... Very well," he says finally, and looses the bag into her hands.

She doesn't look in it. Privacy, and more urgent matters at hand. Instead she sets it in the sink against the far wall, where at least it won't be dripping on the floor anymore, and detours very briefly to flick the lock on the door before returning to her patient.

On closer examination the metal through his leg is an iron bar, pointed on one end, cleanly snapped at the other, as if he's taken part of a fence off in his thigh. She'd dearly like to know precisely how that happened, but blood is already pooling slow and dark beneath it, despite the sealing virtues of keeping the instrument in the wound. Time is rather of the essence.

"It's good you left the bar in place," Rosemary says, grimacing. "That's probably saved your life, honestly. How far did you walk on this?" Does she *want* to know?

"Not terribly far," he says, looking down at it himself. In the bright of these lights, she would speculate it's the first he's seen it clearly, and she's half-expecting him to pass out, but instead there's only a removed curiosity.

Rosemary decides she doesn't believe him, but she will be polite enough in turn to act as if she does until later. "Mmhm," she says neutrally, and goes for scissors.

She cuts his makeshift tourniquet away, then the portions of his pant leg that are immediately in the way. The bar was driven clear through from one side to the other, which means there's a decent chance of fabric still in his leg. She'll have to look before she closes things up.

"I'm going to numb the area," she says, laying thoughts and process in order at once. Forceps are to hand; she pulls the lamp overhead down a little more to shed brighter light on the problem. Again a vague wistful thought for the fact she had to consciously turn away from light magic; it would be so *useful* sometimes. "Then pull the bar out. The most you should feel once I start working is cold, and a tug."

"Don't let me stop you," he says. There's a dryness in his tone that speaks well for his composure. "I'll just bleed a little more, if you don't mind."

"Your arteries likely don't care if I mind," Rosemary murmurs, unable to quite resist even as she's setting fingertips to his bare thigh. One breath; two breaths; *push*. Energy moves through her to him, laying out the internal details. Seeing is not the problem: seeing what's important is. She isolates the nerves in the immediate area, blocks any signals sent upward with quick, efficient mental touches.

"Ah," says the stranger, and now he sounds pleasantly surprised. "That *is* better."

She wonders, absently, if he's been magically healed before. Hard to say how old he is. Rosemary keeps her left hand where it is on his thigh, steady, and takes firm hold of the bar with her right. "Three," she says distantly, "Two." She doesn't bother with one, only pulls.

The iron comes free with a terrible squelching sound. As it does blood tries to flow into the opened space, hot and unrestricted, but within a second Rosemary has control of the blood vessels as well, providing a temporary seal of her own. She drops the bar off to the side and snags up the forceps, peering into the hole left behind.

Her focus is now split three ways, with the result that when the stranger says something further, she doesn't at all hear it. Instead she bends her head out of the light and starts picking out errant fragments of cloth. Doesn't need to be perfect, but the more she leaves behind, the more work she has to do magically.

Between the light and the fact that two-thirds of her awareness is dedicated to the finer workings of his leg, Rosemary manages to get what she thinks is most of the foreign material. It's good enough to be getting on with, anyway, and means she can turn her attention to the healing.

This part is mostly connections, and making them. Where blood vessels have been severed, she aligns them with quick nudges, starts the growth process again. With each step she withdraws a little more, until she's encouraging skin to lay down a quick beginning layer. He's not fully healed, not by a long shot, but as long as he's careful with it ...

The last step is to give him feeling back. Rosemary cheats here, just a little — she leaves a touch of her magic along the nerves, not enough to completely block feeling, only dull it some. It will fade sooner rather than later. Pain is a good warning that the body will not tolerate something; she'd just like a few things answered from a clear mind before she sets him up to rest.

When she looks up, he's watching her. He's pale, but that seems like his natural complexion, and he isn't shaking or fever-flushed. Good. "Have you been healed magically before?" she asks, now that she's not immediately trying to patch him up.

"Once or twice, a while ago." His answer could be less helpful, but Rosemary struggles to see how.

"Then I'll refresh your memory." She tucks her hair back behind one ear — there's a warm damp streak, and she shoves off the urge to curse as she realises she still has his blood on at least one hand. She can freeze out any risk of any contagion, it's just — annoying.

"Please do." He's courteous as he inclines his head to her, and then bends to examine her work.

Rosemary talks over her shoulder as she goes to wash her hands, shifting his bag in the sink aside. The scent there is stronger now, and glass clinks again, almost crunching. "Magical healing uses my resources and yours. What I've done is help your body align itself and fed you enough power to get the process started at speed. You're going to be hungry, and I recommend high-protein meals for at least the next two days. Drink more than you think you need to." She pitches her voice to carry over the running water.

The liquid from the bag is translucent red. Not dark enough to be blood, but a leading colour. Hm.

"It's also not completely healed yet." She could, in truth, but she doesn't know him and she's not exhausting herself on a stranger's mysterious injury. "It will continue to heal faster than you normally do if you support the processes, but in the meantime you need to be careful. Keep your weight off it as much as possible, and —"

She turns away from the sink to dry her hands, and catches sight of the man attempting to stand, braced on his cane. Automatically, Rosemary scowls. Rash, impatient mages who think they know better than healers will eventually get her arrested for murder. At least this one has the bare minimum of sense to use the cane. "*Sit down*," she says.

He leans back against the table, breathing heavily, and offers her the same charming smile he tried when he first came in. It's a better effort this time, his face not so lined with pain. Rosemary notes now, a little further removed from blood and urgency, that he's handsome enough in his tall and dark way, and the tailoring and cloth of his suit are much better than she customarily sees.

All academic right now, as he's attempting to be very stupid. "If you continue to move, you may well tear it open again," Rosemary says, more sharply. "And this time I'm tempted to invoice you before I do anything about it."

"I'm afraid I don't have the luxury of resting this evening," the stranger says. At least he's still being polite. "I will *try* to be careful. I should hate to make you think I have no appreciation for your work, Healer ...?"

"Ingram," she says, and would say more, but there's the bell from over the front door, and she is suddenly uncomfortably aware that the waiting room looks like the prelude to a murder scene. She holds up one finger at him: *wait*. "I need to deal with my guest. I recommend you stay here, *seated*, and give some thought to your feelings on bleeding out."

"I make no promises," he says dryly, but subsides for now at least to lean against the table. Rosemary will take it.

She heads back out the way she came. It proves to be Ms Reed at the door, alarmed at the mess but healthy enough, and Rosemary breathes out a sigh of relief, letting go of some tension. "There you are," she says, stepping over a blood spatter. "Is everything all right?"

"Just fine," Ms Reed says. "I had to stay late at work, and there was some sort of traffic accident on the way here — delayed the bus — I didn't realise I was quite so late, or I would have called."

"It's all right," Rosemary tells her, trying not to think of the stranger in the operating room. "Why don't you come into my office, and I'll see how you're doing? It shouldn't take us too long."

Ms Reed looks down, rather obviously, at the bloodstains, and then back up at Rosemary. "If there's an emergency, I can wait ..."

"All taken care of now, save the clean-up," Rosemary says briskly, trying to believe it. "Please don't worry."

"All right." There's just some little further hesitation — blood on the waiting-room floor really inspires confidence in no one — and then Ms Reed steps carefully around it, purse held tight to herself as if it will shield her. Rosemary takes her to her office, and falls into the easy rhythm of their standard adaptation appointment, magic on her fingertips and calming words in her mouth. Mostly she manages to put the stranger from her mind for the moment; but the moment only ever lasts so long.

THREE

TO RENT A SKELETON

Kian watches Healer Ingram exit and promptly moves to straighten up, testing his leg very gingerly. A hiss escapes him: no, he's not likely to be able to walk far without tearing something open; he can feel the way muscle moves, and on a more magical level the sluggishness of dying limb being fortified with blood-flow once more. Perhaps the good healer can be bribed to provide more thorough healing. He's not precisely lacking for money, though he'll be lacking more if she only takes cash, as some of these small clinics do.

His leg tingles, and he can't quite tell if that's blood returning to his foot or the sense of her magic in his tissue. Light-aligned, certainly; he's never been healed by someone light-aligned until now. Most healers are water-aligned or alchemists: the alchemists naturally use that to succeed with a mundane doctorate and turn out rich, while the water-aligned healers simply have a 'knack' and wind up in clinics for the common people. Light-aligned mages as healers work on connections of philosophy and belief rather than pragmatics. It's the more difficult route.

It's also making the inside of his thigh itch, like his leg's been immersed in freezing water and is only now thawing.

Nevertheless. First Kian reaches for the scissors left on the trolley to cut off a piece of his trousers, an act which takes more time and pain than he could wish, owing to needing to twist. Then he moves, because if he's going to be lectured he may as well do the crime beforehand; and he's thankful now that he *has* an aesthetic for canes, because certainly it's coming in useful. If only he'd been able to draw the blade inside and stab someone with it, without losing the organs.

The bag is still in the sink, red-translucent fluids pooling at the bottom. Kian steadies himself by leaning hip against counter and not putting weight on his bad leg, and unzips the top so he can assess the damage. One of the jars is unbroken: the rest are in various states of it, and if he puts in his hand he's likely to be cut. Wonderful.

He does not put in his hand; he finds a sieved plug for the sink and tips it all, as carefully as he can manage, into the basin — except for the unbroken jar, which he removes on its own to set on the counter. Organs ooze, formalin stinks, and glass tinkles; and once in the sink he empties the unbroken jar and turns on the tap to wash them all, risking his fingers to turn over organs until he's satisfied the smaller pieces of glass and the formalin have been washed away.

When he'd been cajoled into performing this errand, Kian had at least had the foresight to ask what kind of music his dearly-departed colleague liked. Johnny Cash is an interesting choice, for a necromancer, but there's no accounting for tastes of the soul. Kian twists the strip of fabric from his trousers until blood grudgingly starts to drip, whistling *Folsom Prison Blues*, which is the only Johnny Cash song he knows well enough for it; and in the sink, the organs quiver, the heart flops over, the lungs expand ever so slightly. The warmth in them is like a flutter of non-existent pulse, the warmth of maybe-life as opposed to grill.

"*What* do you think you're doing?!" Healer Ingram demands sharply from the doorway, and Kian holds up a finger, neither turning toward her nor halting the whistle.

There's a skeleton against the wall, wired and hanging and marked with various coloured inks — a pragmatic and immediate reference for broken limbs, surely. Carelessly Kian flicks his fingers in its direction, flinging blood off and splattering the bones. The organs quiver again, and in a sudden stir of movement leap onto the counter's edge and tumble down to the floor, bounding across tile like a pack of gruesomely rambunctious puppies leaving a trail of blood and water behind.

Kian never really gets tired of seeing a set of intestines slither their way into crevices, liver flapping in-between ribs — though, to be fair, it wouldn't be something they could do unless a crevice were made for them. Organs really only stir themselves to independent movement if the allure of *fitting* is strong enough. Within seconds the organs have situated themselves comfortably, if not entirely supported, inside the skeleton's cavities; the lungs, in particular, brace themselves against the inside of the ribs so as not to fall onto everything else, and the heart flops against them like a lazy cat sprawled across its owner.

The skeleton stirs, the head jerks, and one arm reaches up to unlatch itself from the stand, hitting the floor with a clatter of wired bone.

"Good morning, Gregory," Kian tells it cheerfully. "*Please* tell me you remember dying. I do so hate to have to remind the deceased that they're dead." The skeleton's jawbone clacks but nothing comes out, and though eye-sockets are empty the way it looks in his direction seems offended. Kian sighs. "This is hardly my fault. Someone stole your corpse from the morgue. You *do* know where it is, I hope?"

The skeleton's jawbone clacks again, and its phalanges rattle as it taps its neck furiously. "Oh, please, it's not exactly standard procedure for autopsies to remove the larynx," Kian says with exasperation. "What, dancing an interpretative jig will kill you?" The skeleton folds its arms and turns its skull away, and Kian rolls his eyes. "*Necromancers.*" Post-death snobs. He reserves his rights to cast judgement on his peers.

Kian turns, awkwardly owing to his leg throbbing madly, and smiles brightly. "Healer Ingram! I don't suppose you have a model of a larynx and some intravenous tubing?"

Ingram's gaze is on Gregory, or rather Gregory inhabiting her skeleton; and to her credit her face is more about fascinated startle than it is disgust, shock or something Kian otherwise does not have time or inclination to manage. The streak of blood is still on her cheek — that's pragmatically endearing, if she's forgotten about it — and her hair is still behind her definably pointed ear. So, light-aligned *and* at least partially elfin. No wonder her hair's luminescent. That also explains the Welsh-mixed-Cockney in her accent, particularly if half-elfin; notoriously bloodline-centric, they are, and most on this particular isle are in Wales.

"No," she answers slowly, unblinking. "That's not something I habitually — you can't simply *take my skeleton*."

"Borrowing," Kian assures her quickly. "*Renting*, if you'd like to add it to the invoice." He'll expense it to the church when he asks whether they'd known Gregory was murdered, not merely dead. "It was a touch urgent; someone tried to kill me tonight and I'd rather like to know why." The skeleton rattles furiously, and Kian adds smoothly, "And finding out who murdered you too, Gregory, of course. That would happen much more smoothly if you'd be willing to tap something out for me."

Gregory gives him a two-fingered salute, and Kian sighs. Just goes to show how rude younger clerics have become these days. Honestly, do they even *teach* basic metrical linguistics these days? Maybe he's refusing because he can't.

"Did this attempted assassination involve a vehicle?" Ingram asks, which is frankly the last thing Kian expects, until he recalls the unnamed guest and the likelihood of someone having to pass Tower Hill Road to get here. The police are more than likely at the scene by now.

"It did, as a matter of fact; a vehicle, myself, and the wrought-iron fence lining the Tower of London."

"You walked here from the Tower of London?" Ingram demands sharply, and Kian holds up a finger.

"Trinity Square," he corrects. "Shadow-stepping is not precisely common, and can be devilishly hard, but fortunately I'm more than up to the task given an appropriately powerful deathspring in the vicinity."

She presses a hand to her eyes and then folds them, her mouth a delightfully flat line undeterred by either possessed skeleton or the slime trail left by Gregory's organs from the sink. "Is this likely to get my clinic into trouble?"

"I don't see why it would," Kian admits. "It's not as if you're involved, and most people willing to kill others are still loathe to draw attention by rampantly murdering healers." Communities tend to spring up around certain kinds of people, and healers are one of them. "The larynx?"

Ingram shakes her head. "I have nothing like that — the larynx, anyway. I have some tubing."

"It won't do without something on the end, I'm afraid." Kian regards Gregory's stiff belligerence, considering. "Would you happen to have some spare sets of clothes? Scrubs, perhaps?"

"Well, yes," answers Ingram cautiously. "I'd like them back, but if they'll get you as far as home I can last without them a few days."

"Oh, not for me," Kian assures her, and then pauses, plucking crossly at his ruined trousers. "Not *only* for me. I'm afraid Gregory can't be wandering around the streets like that."

"*My skeleton* can't be wandering around the streets at all," Ingram answers sharply, crossing her arms. "It's *my* skeleton."

Kian considers and discards a reminder of money, and opts for generously: "You *can* come with."

"Come with to *where?*"

"Wherever Gregory's corpse is," Kian answers, "at which point I can de-animate the skeleton and return the organs, or at the very least remove them from the skeleton for you. And I *would*, of course, pay for the rental of the skeleton."

She gives him a disbelievingly calculating look, which says much for her pragmatism: not so willing to dismiss some additional income just for the absurdity of the situation. Well, absurd for someone who isn't a necromancer, anyway; so far she's held up well.

"*You* aren't in the condition to go wandering around the streets either," she reminds him.

"I'll pay you extra for additional healing," he offers, and smiles winsomely. "Or I'll just continue to walk about on my cane and with an exceedingly thin friend to support me, and who knows what will happen?"

"Don't make *me* responsible for *your* irresponsibility," she snaps, which is a fair enough accusation given how Kian's felt about the irresponsibility of his colleagues; thus, Kian holds up a hand in concession.

"Fair enough. Bribery it is, then. Well?"

Ingram looks at him, at the skeleton, at the blood on the table, and sighs. "Sit down. I still can't heal you the whole way, but I suppose I can stand a little more."

"Excellent." Kian points to the blood on the stainless-steel top as he shifts to limp, very carefully and gingerly, back. "By the by, I don't suppose you can put whatever's left of that in a jar for me? It'll be useful if I need to extend the animation bond, and there's no point in opening a vein when all that's just laying around unable to be used for anything else."

Ingram eyes it and fetches a container while he makes his way across the floor — as well as a towel to clean up with. "I suppose it's better than you deliberately bleeding for it," she says grudgingly. "Do you have a name, or do I just call you 'Pastor'?"

"Cleric," Kian corrects, "though frankly it makes me sound like a stuffy old theologian; my name is Kian ó Maolomhnaigh." He watches her try to sound out the intensely Irish sounds, allowing only a trace of smugness show in his smile. She shakes her head as he lifts himself awkwardly back onto the table, wiping down the stainless steel.

"Irishmen," she mutters, setting down a vial of half-congealed blood scraped from the table; it'll do, at least for the next few hours. Reanimations don't particularly care if blood is contaminated. "All right; hold still."

Her magic feels as it had before: like frost growing from the outside in, the harsh glare of sunlight with edges but no heat. It feels extra cutting to him, necromancers frequently being dark-aligned, and darkness generally being warm. It might feel

25

worse, if not for the fact she deadens the nerves beforehand, just like she had before; and isn't that an additional touch he somehow hadn't expected of a clinic healer? The weave on her wall is more than earned, it seems.

When Ingram straightens and steps back Kian steps down from the table only carefully, testing leg and weight on it. It pangs but holds; with cane and walking slowly, he should be able to manage.

"You're going to be hungry soon, after that," she warns, turning toward the door. "If we can, we should try to get something to eat on the way."

In the inner city, there's no lack for food this late at night, if not the sort Kian customarily prefers; he bows shallowly nonetheless. "Of course, Healer Ingram. Allow me to treat you, for the inconvenience."

She makes a noise which could be either non-committal or a snort, and Kian hears her rummaging in a closet in the hall before returning with some clothes draped over her arms, which she sets down on the counter nearest Gregory which has not, of late, been covered in blood and fluids. "Here. I'm going to go clean up the waiting-room; come out when you're ready."

She leaves again and draws the door almost-closed behind her, giving them some privacy. Or, well, Kian some privacy. Gregory finally unwinds a little and looks at Kian with an ever-grinning skull, and taps his nose-hole. Kian rolls his eyes. "Oh, please; *do* be less crass."

That is all he's going to say on *that* matter. He turns his back, quite deliberately, and leaves Gregory to figure out how to dress himself. The trousers are done for; his socks possibly too. The shoes are potentially saveable, if this doesn't take long. Kian gets shoes off first, then socks, shaking and twisting any excess blood into the jar Ingram had provided; and that ought to be more than enough to keep the reanimation going for his purposes. He does at least spare himself a quick rundown with the towel, at least so he won't be as likely to get the scrubs dirty ... if they can be called scrubs. They look more like sweatpants. Kian eyes them for only a moment before grudgingly conceding that beggars can't be choosers. Still, he's not happy to pull them on, nor his damp socks and stained shoes; and by the time he turns around Gregory is at least somewhat dressed, in sweats and hoodie and a pair of bright-yellow wellies.

Kian very graciously does not laugh. "It'll do."

Gregory divines his amusement anyway and attempts to sweep out of the room in a definite huff, stumbling over wellies and the lack of actual flesh and substance inside them. Kian follows, leaning on his cane and buttoning his coat so it at least isn't terribly obvious his suit is no longer a suit; and when they emerge into the waiting-room Healer Ingram is already by the door, aloofly impatient now she's apparently decided the best thing for her to do is keep them on the straight and narrow — if only for her skeleton's sake.

FOUR

FOOD FOR THE SOUL

Rosemary doesn't anticipate she'll have time for a full and proper sanitising before Kian and Gregory are ready to go. She opts for a quick clean, since she would have been closing up around this time anyway, and she'll come back and do a proper quality job when she has her skeleton back. She doesn't bother with a coat, only drapes her scarf across her shoulders once she's done the first round of getting blood up, and then finds herself waiting for Kian *anyway*.

She wishes he'd say his surname a few more times where she can hear it. She's managed Latin names for every part of the body, she can manage *one* Irish surname with a few more vowels than is strictly necessary, and she's not about to let this be the thing to stop her.

There's no good way to ask at this point, however, and they rather have larger problems. She grimaces faintly as Kian and

Gregory emerge into the waiting room, one still limping notably, the other almost stumbling in the boots. This is one of the worse ideas she's had lately. "After you," she says, gesturing to the door. "I need to lock up."

The bell rings as they go, the scent of blood in their wake weaker than it had been but still notable. Sighing, Rosemary flicks the lights and locks the door.

She turns in time to see Gregory tripping up the stairs to the street. "*Careful*," she says sharply. She can't repair non-living bone herself, and having the skeleton as reference tool and template has been frankly invaluable, especially in the early months of her tenure here.

There may be a slight sentimental attachment.

The streets aren't as busy as they would be during the day, but they're not fully deserted either, even at the delightful hour of half-past four in the morning. Rosemary eyes Gregory with some mild concern — finally unloops her scarf and takes a few quick steps toward him, leaning up to drape it over his shoulders. "Use that to hide your face," she instructs.

The skull turns fractionally, eye sockets pointing toward her. It's both fascinating and unnerving to see focus where there can't possibly be any. Rosemary has a distinct feeling Gregory is unamused, and the prickle across her shoulders has her scowling at the macabre grin.

"Whenever you're ready, Gregory," Kian says, with the sort of politeness that sounds only a veneer. "Lead the way. We don't *actually* have all night."

The skeleton straightens up, turning this way and that. Rosemary pushes her hands into her pockets, fidgeting vaguely with the pen in one of them as she waits.

"Do remember it would be advisable to stop for food," she says after a moment, as Gregory picks a direction. She's never seen a body start to consume muscle for fuel yet, and she frankly doesn't feel like tonight is an optimal time to find out what it looks like.

Naturally, Gregory's first step is to cross the street at an angle. Kian moves after him, intent, quickly finding a counterpoint between cane and wounded leg that seems to work for him. Rosemary doesn't quite trail, but she brings up the rear, frowning bitterly. "And no jaunts through hedges," she says, under the hope that she's going to be listened-to.

Kian lifts his free hand to acknowledge this, turning an amused glance on her over his shoulder. "Your concern is duly noted, Healer Ingram. I shall endeavour to contain myself."

Somehow, Rosemary doesn't completely believe him.

"Why don't you fill in the details of how you got into this state in the first place," she says, quickening her step until she's more or less abreast of him. If she can't keep up with a wounded man, even given the disparity in the length of their legs, she'll be disappointed in herself. "You mentioned an assassination attempt."

"Much of it is still a mystery," Kian says, which mostly sounds like a justification for not explaining. "You did say you were concerned about repercussions on your clinic, did you not?"

"I doubt just knowing things is liable to bring harm," she says crisply. "If it was, I'm sure I would have died long before I achieved any sort of degree. Right now, I need more data. So please: elaborate."

Gregory pauses at the intersection, turns left after some short deliberation. Rosemary isn't sure if she's actually hearing the faint rattle-and-squish from his steps, or only imagining them because she expects a skeleton with a few organs packed into its pitiful thoracic cavity to make rather more noise.

Those clothes will definitely need laundering.

"I was serious about the relative mystery," Kian says after another moment. "I was — asked — to collect Gregory's remains, and was informed that he had already been autopsied and his corpse removed. It was luck the coroner still had the organs. Shortly after that, someone tried to kill me. There, now you're caught up."

Rosemary resists the urge to rub her temples. That's no more than he's already said, just put differently. This is the opposite of elaborating. "The vehicle incident. So you said. Was there *nothing* else?"

"A mage." Their reasonable pace carries them along. Another intersection, this one with a complicated mess of crosswalks. Gregory opts against these, turning with the street. "Water, showing as ice. It's unclear if there was anything else. I was a little, shall we say, distracted."

"By the attempted murder," Rosemary fills in. "Yes, I'm aware." This is a great deal of nothing. Poor grounds for a fool's errand across the city in the wee hours of the morning, and yet the alternative is to allow him to simply walk off with her skeleton.

"There you have it, then."

Perhaps he's *trying* to be infuriating, now that charm hasn't precisely worked for him. Under other circumstances it might have. Maybe. Rosemary isn't in the habit of attraction to gaping wounds, however. "You've been very helpful," she informs him, as frigidly as she knows how.

Kian smiles at her. "I try," he says.

He's trying. Rosemary looks away, keeps an eye on the people and surrounds like she should have been doing anyway. Gregory isn't that far ahead of them, walking like he's got somewhere to be. His gait is erratic for all his purpose, though — with any luck, the people around them will take him for drunk.

She doubts most humans will assume there's a skeleton walking among them.

"There," Rosemary says, at the next intersection, and she points across. Fast food. Hardly the best of health, but someplace open at this time, and good for acquiring many calories very quickly. "We're stopping there." Gregory can be sat in a corner, and with any luck no one will look too closely. The hour works in their favour yet again.

Kian takes one look at the distinctive golden arches and grimaces very visibly. "Surely there's some other option."

"It's on the way." Rosemary folds her arms. "Is that animation a constant drain or a one-time expenditure? If the latter, how long until you need to renew it? Because doubtless you'll need energy for either one of those possibilities, as well as for the healing. I'm almost surprised I haven't heard your stomach yet."

She will admit to herself that there is some pettiness at work here; that she wouldn't be insisting on precisely *this* restaurant if Kian was not being so picky about his options. She spent her share of time and money on fast food during medical school, and while it might be a nostalgia filled with sleepless nights and bitter black coffee, in a pinch the nutrients are just as solid as any other.

"Somewhere between those," Kian says, relenting a little. "It doesn't take much *energy* to keep going, but a constant supply of blood, the necessary volume of which is determined by what is being animated, and what is demanded of it. Gregory, here, is only a collection of organs right now, which is not very much — but by the same token it requires more effort for lungs and heart and intestines to get up and walk." He looks between the restaurant and Rosemary herself, and she can see the effort it takes to put a cheerful expression on. "Very well. I did promise to treat you, did I not?"

Gregory rattles irritably. Kian turns his head toward him. "Take it up with the good Healer," he says, with a brittle sort of affability. "She seems convinced I'd be happy to run myself to collapse following your body."

It's sarcasm, of course it is, but Rosemary isn't convinced he wouldn't. He seems like precisely the sort of person who has little regard for his own safety — that is, the sort of person it will be difficult for her to help in the long term, unless some change is made. She doesn't know him well enough yet to say if talking him into looking after himself will be worth the necessary effort. "I will be happy to be convinced otherwise," she says primly, and points at the restaurant. "By eating."

The lights inside are bright. Probably they seem brighter than they actually are, given the dark of the sky. All the same, it makes Rosemary cast a few nervous glances at Gregory. She concludes her own reactions to him are more likely to make him seem suspicious, given the way the hood is drawn up and the scarf pulled up over his face, but somehow this doesn't make her much less concerned.

"Why don't you order, and I'll secure a corner seat," Rosemary says aloud finally. She almost reaches for Gregory — debates — and then actually does catch loosely at his arm, taking hold of sleeve instead of bone. The dead man tugs back; Rosemary scowls at him, and imagines he would do similarly if he could. For a man who can't speak, Gregory is rapidly making a sub-par impression on her. "Order at least twice as much as you would ordinarily."

"Hm." Kian seems to consider this. Rosemary bites her tongue — it's no good snapping a man's head off for things he hasn't said, and she likes to be even-handed. "Very well. Any preferences?"

How fortunate. Rosemary shakes her head in the negative. "I'm not picky," she says, and pulls at Gregory until he follows her. There's a four-person table tucked away around the corner from the register, where it's a little darker and also out of direct line-of-sight. She watches with some fascination as Gregory navigates the art of sitting down, and then herself takes up a seat opposite him.

Rosemary has several things to ruminate over — what it must feel like to be separate from and drawn to your own body, what act of dubious charm Kian will next find appropriate, how much energy it will take her to re-generate blood if he runs low and more practical long-term solutions for that problem. She watches Gregory fidget and wishes she'd had the foresight to bring gloves — well, not that they would have stayed on.

Something occurs between one thought and the next, as skeletal fingers trigger some problem-solving instincts. Rosemary sits up straight. "Could you write?" she asks hopefully. "I'm aware mime or Morse code are out of the question, but do you have the manual dexterity to write anything down?"

Gregory stills at this, head tilted to one side. After a moment he offers her a hand, palm-up, beckoning.

She does have a pen in her pocket. Rosemary digs it out, puts it into his hand. The next several minutes are spent agreeably watching Gregory try to get a good grip on the pen. A standard grip doesn't work for him, and a fist turns out to be too loose, without the mass and friction of muscle and tendon and skin. The pen skitters out of his hand once or twice.

He's got it awkwardly braced between two fingers finally when Kian joins them, setting down a tray near to overflowing with food. "Your burgers, Healer Ingram," he says dryly. "Napkin, Gregory?"

The pen catches on napkin, but Gregory does manage something: a shaky-lined sketch of a rude gesture.

Rosemary rubs at her eyes, sighs, and takes the pen back before anything further profane can be produced. "It was worth a try."

"It was," Kian agrees brightly. "What you have to understand is that Gregory *wants* to be whole. More than he wants to be helpful to us. Not to mention that, depending on where he is, he may not be able to perceive much of anything. Following the pull to the rest of himself is now the most efficient option."

"Even 'dark' or 'near the river' would do for a start," Rosemary mutters, and reaches for food.

There's something delightfully surreal about the previously finely-dressed necromancer unwrapping a burger to tuck into it with delicate precision. And once Kian's started, as Rosemary predicted, he doesn't slow down, for all his earlier distaste at the concept of fast food. Halfway through he does pause, but it's only because Gregory is starting to slump over the table. Kian uncaps the container of blood from earlier — Rosemary winces with some thought for food-handling regulations — and with quick flicks of his fingers and a few notes of a whistle, a good portion of the vial has disappeared under Gregory's hood.

The skeleton sits up straighter. Rosemary eats and thinks. Conversation is mostly stalled in favour of efficient consumption, and Gregory seems impatient now that he's been roused again. Perhaps it would have been wiser to wait to reinforce the magic — then again, perhaps it would have been a larger expenditure to renew it fresh, and Rosemary also doesn't like to think of the animated organs subsiding into an untidy pile.

Three employees have passed by giving them dubious looks under pretence of cleaning. Rosemary had believed the first one, but they don't need three people for one spill, and she's well aware they look a strange group. "Why don't we take the last with us," Rosemary says, rising before they're strictly done.

"There's no need to leave early on their account." Kian seems unconcerned, which is a turnabout for someone who earlier hadn't wanted to be here at all. Rosemary concludes he simply has a contrary nature. "You were the one urging us to eat, Healer Ingram. I'm only following orders."

The looks from the employees are making her shoulders itch. Rosemary tucks her hair back — remembers the shape of her ears — draws it forward with some brief frustration. "The fewer times you need to refresh the magic on Gregory, the better."

Kian remains unconcerned. Rosemary remains standing. They don't leave the restaurant for another ten minutes, while Kian takes his time, apparently out of sheer spite.

Clearly his personality is why he's cultivated a charming smile.

FIVE

WHERE CANARIES DON'T SING

H ealer Ingram, Kian decides, is far more uptight than she looks. Or perhaps too honest. Three bored food-service retailers find excuses to ogle the weirdos out at four in the morning, and she gets antsy. It's an odd dichotomy given that she, as a magical being, has much more to hide. Kian's amused enough to keep the faint indulgent smile on his face, despite the fact that his leg aches and his mouth now tastes of processed burgers. If he hadn't just been healed twice over he would never have walked into such a place; but he can be, and in fact frequently is, pragmatic.

Gregory lurches from street to street, and Kian would be more concerned about keeping up except that the wellies quite easily keep Gregory down to a perpetually stumbling trip. On the flipside, dawn can't be much longer than an hour away, and the earliest risers have started to come out of the city's woodwork. Cars become more common on the streets as they pass; and in the end, all Kian can think is that he ought to have known.

Canary Wharf rises ahead of them, already lit. Probably there's already any number of people working — janitors, bakers, chefs, early risers. Kian pauses under a streetlight only to fish for his pocketwatch, and returns it when Ingram pauses to check on him. Gregory doesn't pause at all. In fact, he seems to be speeding up.

"Are you alright?" Ingram asks, so Kian bestows upon her one of his cheerful-charming smiles.

"Perfectly." Aside from the throb in his leg, the ache in his temples, and the general feeling of malaise which comes from either having bled a little too much for the amount of exercise he's getting, or having eaten something disagreeable. Perhaps both. At least healing-hunger means the food doesn't have a chance to sit in his stomach. "Depending on where Gregory is taking us, however, we may run into people likely to ask whether we have a right to be present. Ordinarily this would not be a problem for me, but I'm hardly properly dressed."

If they're lucky he can stick well enough to the shadows to hide that his pants are not trousers, nor even remotely close to the right shade.

"Is this where the necromancers live?" Ingram asks with a nod ahead to the Wharf, and Kian laughs before he can attempt to modulate, or decide if he wants to. He probably wouldn't have.

"No, not at all," he answers. "Most necromancers wouldn't be caught *dead* here." In the distance, Gregory turns to give him a rude gesture with *both* hands, and Kian laughs again, and does not think he's misjudging the twitch at Ingram's mouth before she smooths it. "It's too far from Tower Hill," Kian explains. "Or so I've been told. No, I imagine any mages here are the sort with too much ambition — or just enough of it, depending on your perspective. The trouble is that this place has far better security."

"I assume breaking and entering isn't on the agenda," says Ingram primly.

"Oh, let's not make assumptions, shall we?" Kian says cheerfully, and nods ahead. "Besides, the closer we get, the more compelled Gregory will be to find his body. We may not be able to stop him." They may have already passed that point, given Gregory stumbles onto Westferry Circus with hardly a glance. Kian winces as a car screeches to a halt with a blast of horn, and they both hurry their step. Ingram gets there first: Kian leaves her to handle the driver while Kian wraps an arm around Gregory's back, propping him up and covering for his narrowness at once, and chivvying him past the roundabout as quickly as possible. Ingram hurries to catch up as they get beyond the road, and by that point Kian is carrying nearly the weight of both of them on the cane.

"The jar, if you please," he grunts, but Ingram goes instead for Gregory, propping him up between her shoulder and the wall. That'll do; Kian fishes in his pocket for the jar and pours a little more of his blood into his hand, and flicks that while whistling under the hood. Gregory shakes himself and straightens up, and thankfully Kian doesn't hear the sound of organs hitting the ground under him. He does wish Gregory turned before he reaches under the hoodie to pull up his kidneys; but rather than say anything, Kian chooses merely to stopper the jar and wipe off his fingers on his handkerchief. At this point his hand's going to start smelling, which is absolutely fantastic. He does so hate having to work with old blood, but he really can't afford to lose any more.

Gregory yanks himself away from Ingram and takes off, moving at a faster, still stumbling pace. Kian motions ahead of him. "Get him to lean on you if you can."

They can move faster than he can, currently; and even trying to keep up from a distance is making his leg throb harder. Nevertheless he perseveres — up until Gregory vanishes suddenly around a corner, and Rosemary does likewise a startled moment later.

"Oh, wonderful," Kian mutters, and increases his pace to something a generous person might call 'ill-advised'. He makes the corner just about when Gregory throws himself against a locked 'staff' door with a dull rattling thud.

"Stop that," Rosemary orders, getting in front of him, and Gregory almost bowls her over trying to go at it again.

"Allow me," says Kian, not out of breath but very definitely limping, and Gregory only barely restrains himself, rattling impatiently as Kian tugs on a glove and sets hand to lock and filters shadow into it, filling the whole of the space until anything that *can* move, *must*. The lock clicks and Kian pushes the door open, and Gregory shoves past. Kian bites down on a pained noise and brushes off his coat, and extends an arm courteously to Ingram. "After you, Healer Ingram. You see? No 'breaking' necessary."

"For spirits' sakes," she mutters as she follows, chin lifted and head straight, and yet grimace still on mouth. Kian closes the door quietly and locks it again with a tiny thread of shadow, and then follows, grimacing himself when his leg complains. That does not feel good in the least.

"Perhaps we should have put a leash on him," he says, for no other reason than to pretend he's not having as much trouble as he is, and succeeding only in having Ingram look over her shoulder, her eyes glinting weirdly in the dim light. The effect is lost when she frowns.

"You've hurt yourself," she says disapprovingly, and pauses at the corner to wait for him.

"Nothing's re-opened," Kian assures her. He's just very thankful for his cane right now. "Best keep moving, or we'll both lose him. I assume the last thing you want is to have your skeleton found clothed and with a pile of organs."

She continues to look disapproving, but after a moment nods and resumes, hurrying to catch up to Gregory just vanishing around another corner. Kian follows at a more practical speed, and thanks God when there's service lifts instead of merely stairs. He's fairly sure the good healer would have left him at the bottom, if that had been the case.

Up and up they go, and the only reason Kian keeps up is because Gregory needs to be yanked into a lift, and then Ingram proceeds to hold the doors for Kian himself, with Gregory jiggling impatiently beside her. They must've gone around the tower twice just while Gregory circles trying to find the best way in; eventually, finally,

Kian stops at the service lift, holding the door open and pointing down the hall for them to get out. "I believe we can assume Gregory's body is somewhere on this floor or the ones just below or above," he says dryly. "There's no point in going round and round."

Gregory glares; or at least Kian is good enough at reading skulls to guess at there being a glare. Kian points again, gesturing with his cane. "Don't sulk, there's a good boy. You keep going up and over, down and around. Clearly what you're after is somewhere in the middle. That means we'll need to leave the service corridors."

"I believe that door may lead out." Ingram points to the one she means, unmarked and grey-toned and lacking any kind of sign — unlike the exits, storage closets, and bathrooms.

"I believe you're correct." When Kian tests the knob it's unlocked, and that more than anything tells him that Gregory is hardly thinking correctly, in as far as he can think at all when Kian had not bothered to negotiate too hard for the brain, given his experience with the difficulty re-installing them. Reanimations can generally think only as far as their soul remembers thinking — and now all Gregory can think is to be reunited with his body.

Kian manages to get through before Gregory pushes him over doing so himself, and so Kian isn't *too* far behind as Ingram catches up and they both follow Gregory down the tastefully-decorated hall to an equally tastefully-decorated door, passing a number of others on the way. There's no windows into the room; it's not that sort of office space, apparently. To the side of the door there's a simple plaque reading *Timothy Carruthers, Business Advisory*, which could frankly mean any number of things.

"If you please, Cleric," says Ingram softly, motioning, and Kian restrains a laugh to a smile, and covers the lock. Within seconds it turns, and before Kian can really attempt to discern whether there's someone on the other side of it, Gregory rushes in.

Thankfully, there *is* no one on the other side of it; simply a small-to-moderately sized office with automated lights, still tastefully furnished but tastefully furnished in the same way as the halls outside. The desk is broad and timber, the bookcases are dusted and neatly aligned. It's something that could have come out of a catalogue, and perhaps did. This is the room of someone who has money, yet chooses to spend it somewhere that isn't on *branding*.

Gregory makes a bee-line directly to those uniform books and yanks out all the ones on a good two-by-one-foot space — precisely the space of one of the shelves. While Ingram makes sure the door is closed Kian limps up behind him, scanning the edges; it takes two passes before he can see the seams where the bookcase has been adhered to wall, and then the lock buried in the case's back. This one is a twisting safe's lock, not a key; thankfully it isn't an electronic one, or they'd be plum out of luck. Kian slaps Gregory's groping hands away and inserts himself in front of the case, leaning on it hip to shoulder and turning his head to listen. The room is quiet as he turns the knob, listening for the tell-tale click, and then click, and then click again — no. Four clicks.

Then a clunk, and the frame loosens, and Kian pulls the door away. Behind there's a whoosh of cold air, and an eminently familiar stainless-steel table laden with corpse which Kian proceeds to pull out. Gregory's shoulders droop, and then straighten, and he taps Kian's shoulder frenetically.

"Do you mind not assaulting me in your impatience?" Kian asks irritably. The easiest thing would be to cut the stitches and instil the organs right away; a skeleton is far lighter to carry than a dead-weight corpse. Leaving a mess might be trouble, though Kian can, he supposes, pluck the organs out of the skeleton's cavity one by one ... which would leave the mess on *Kian* instead, and that's going to be less than fun.

Gregory smacks Kian's shoulder again and motions fumingly at his lower body — his uncovered lower body. Kian rolls his eyes. "Oh, please; she's a healer, I'm sure she's seen many naked men before." Another smack. "I am *not* lending you my coat. You'll just have to settle for getting dressed like an ordinary person, once I've got your organs situated."

Gregory crosses his arms with an extremely rude gesture which Kian proceeds to ignore by turning to Ingram, who looks more amused than he has thus far seen. "If we're lucky there's tools or a body-bag hidden somewhere around here," he tells her. "Anything to put down so I can take the organs out of your skeleton and return them to the corpse. Something sharp, also — I won't need to stitch the organs in, but I will need to cut those stitches."

"It does seem like Mr Carruthers was prepared for a body," Ingram agrees thoughtfully, and that's when the door snicks locked.

Six

ONE CORPSE TOO MANY

Rosemary is much less worried about the modesty problem than the dead man himself — in fact she's wondering, a little, why Gregory is concerned at all. She's seen his organs bare under the fluorescent lights, and surely that's a great deal more personal? A nude man is a nude man, and this one isn't about to be any subject of that sort of interest.

Though it does cause some pause for wondering how much function necromancy restores. After a moment's consideration Rosemary opts not to ask Kian about that. It might be taken poorly. Either that or he'd look unbearably smug. She's known him a few hours and already she wants to give him as few options for that expression as possible.

The *most* pressing issue is wondering why, exactly, one Mr Timothy Carruthers is so prepared to keep bodies in his office that he has a very good freezer built into the wall. Rosemary has not been in very many standard office-buildings, but she has the general understanding that this is not a typical feature, and also probably represents some sort of health hazard.

She's considering this, turning over possible justifications and discarding each as fantastical and unlikely, when she hears something click behind her. That isn't a sound that belongs — not when she had shut the door herself. Alarm prickles down the back of her neck. "Kian," she says. She doesn't know what words are going to come next — warning or question. It's a moot point. Her breath mists as the chill of the freezer spreads, beyond where it should realistically be able to. The bare frost-rime on Gregory's body rises up, becoming something notably solid as it condenses in the air above him.

Water-aligned mage, Rosemary considers, and further that approximately 70% of the human body is composed of water, and that water also lends itself to healing — better, in some ways, than light does. How much water is left in Gregory's corpse and organs, and what is this mage's focus?

She thinks too much. Rosemary is still mid-thought when she's shoved to the side, goes sprawling toward the floor. She catches herself, palms solid against carpet, and glances up immediately, assessing. Gregory-in-the-skeleton is leaning toward Gregory-the-corpse, and doesn't look likely to be distracted any time soon. The skeleton might be slumping, or might be yearning — either way, unhelpful.

The mage is a figure in dark, exercise-tight clothes. Could be a jogger or an assassin. There's a dim-shining blade in their hand which Rosemary takes embarrassingly long to connect to *ice,* and that same blade moves jagged, stitching dull-reflecting blur through the air with the speed it's driven toward Kian.

Kian, who is injured still, and certainly not equipped for rapid dodging. Rosemary's going to have to do something.

He lifts his cane to catch the first strike, and it rebounds, arcs in again. Kian stumbles back, uneven and clearly pained but at least managing to put the heavy wooden desk between him and the assailant. That lasts a second or two — Rosemary pushes herself up to her knees as quietly as she knows how — and then the assassin bounds up onto the desk to pursue. There's an unearthly silence about it all, Kian's ragged breath and sneakers on hardwood somehow the loudest things in the room, louder than the swish of the blade through air and its dull collisions with wood.

Rosemary picks herself up and edges toward the desk, keeping low and quiet. Kian stumbles — there's a pained sound to pair with blade meeting flesh — Rosemary grits her teeth and reminds herself she can fix it. The assassin lifts a leg to kick.

She won't have a better opportunity. Rosemary lunges and snags the mage's supporting leg, getting hands on the strip of skin between sneaker and leggings. Her target flails. No time for narrow precision — she finds a nearby large nerve and deadens it with a thought. It might not be enough. Rosemary reaches for blood vessels, ducks a swinging leg, and then all at once the mage is falling, unsupported, to sprawl across the desk.

On the other side, Kian, bloodied and looking thoroughly unamused about the whole ordeal, reaches for his cane as the assassin pushes themselves up on their elbows. There's a quick flick of his wrist — the top comes loose to reveal a considerable blade. Rosemary braces herself for a cut throat, for the impending wrongness of misaligned blood vessels and liquid in the lungs.

Kian drives the blade straight forward into the mage's eye instead, twists with a terrible precision.

With Rosemary's awareness filtered through the mage's body, she cannot possibly ignore the effects this wreaks. Optical nerves mangled where they aren't severed, bone chips jarred loose of the orbital socket. Electrical impulses in the brain cease, muscles go limp without a centre to command them. Some processes persist — Rosemary tracks a few of them out of habit, automatically trying to hold and sustain a few before she realises what she's doing and pulls herself back, shuddering.

She can't manage the philosophical or moral implications right now. Besides, she can't say herself that she wouldn't have done similarly — though more kindly — if necessary. It's a creative interpretation of the Hippocratic Oath, but she'll stand by it if she must: at worst case, removing the cause of harm is necessary to protect a patient.

She's staring at the corpse. With a deep breath Rosemary picks her gaze up, and she puts the matter away where she can look at it later, and focuses on Kian instead.

Blood-spattered, paler than he was. He pulls the blade free, cleans it meticulously with the edge of the assassin's hoodie. It's the work of some several seconds, and Rosemary finds herself temporarily lulled by the deft, rhythmic movements of his hands.

Kian puts the blade away when it's clean, offers Rosemary a faint smile and short bow over the corpse of their assailant. "Healer Ingram," he says, no less courteously than he ever has. "Might I prevail upon you for further assistance? As necessary as the use of blood is, in these quantities it is, shall we say, wasteful."

"Not to mention dangerous," Rosemary murmurs. It's a little more distant than she likes, potentially giving the lie to the fact that she is just fine for now, thank you. She shakes her head twice, as if that will clear cobwebs and the afterimages of dying neurons from her brain, and then she goes around the desk toward him. Gregory, a quick glance reveals, is now fully collapsed over his body. He might be leaking organ juices. This, too, must be dealt with later. For now: Kian. "It's a good thing I insisted we stop to eat."

"I shall remember to bow to your wisdom in the future," Kian says. It might be an intimate softness if he were not quite so sarcastic. Accordingly, Rosemary ignores him.

The more recent wound has dragged a line down his shoulder, not quite so deep as to hit the clavicle but certainly more than a surface wound. Rosemary leans in to look at it, frowning, tugs the fabric carefully away from the bleeding. It is, at least, a relatively clean cut. "And your leg?"

"I may have jarred it more than advisable," he allows.

"May have." Rosemary sighs pointedly and gustily, having forgotten until she does so precisely how close they are. Ah, well: he's her patient, and handsome means nothing in these circumstances. She toys with asking him to sit down — remembers how much blood he's losing — opts not to grind that into the high-quality desk-chair. This is already crime-scene enough. Instead she just reaches up, works her fingertips into the gap in fabric to bracket the injury firmly.

"May have," he repeats, and offers her an impish sort of grin as she threads her awareness around the wound. Nerves — there. Blood vessels — nudged into alignment. Rosemary feeds power to Kian's own regeneration until it takes over, until bleeding stops and the first vestiges of new skin start to form.

It isn't a great deal. It'll have to do. It *will* do, if they don't run into any other assassins today. It's been long enough since Rosemary slept that she can't summon the immediate hour to mind, and she still has the much-abused leg-wound to contend with. Kian has, as predicted, rather set back the healing, and it's a good thing she did the extra work earlier or it would certainly be bleeding again by now. She shores it up before she withdraws her awareness and steps back, folding her arms.

Maybe she'll amend his invoice to include the increased grocery bill in the offing.

As soon as she's done, Kian starts going through desk drawers, completely ignoring the corpse sprawled over the top. "You don't happen to have a scalpel in your pocket?"

"Only a pen." She can guess at what he's looking for. Rosemary leaves him to it, circling the office with slow, cautious steps. It's ostentatiously minimalist — look at all the space that he can afford to waste! — and the whole thing feels terribly soulless, like not a thing in it is loved, only shown off. The disdain of it makes her lip curl a little, without meaning to. "This room isn't suitable

52

for *doing* anything with a body, and only barely for storing it. It's possible that whatever tools they have are elsewhere."

"And yet they've gone to the trouble to fit this room for storage, when they might have more space and options elsewhere," Kian points out. Two drawers are discarded; he presses his hand to the bottom-most drawer, and there is a series of short clicks as he works the lock over. "The *considerable* trouble. There's at least six feet of space between this room and the next." A pause, to indicate the wall in which the freezer is set, and then he has the drawer out. There's a pleased sound. "Ah. Here we go."

Rosemary completes her circuit, having turned up nothing else out of the ordinary. The books are all trite leadership nonsense and the sort of hardcover classics sets purchased, on the whole, to appear cultured. Most unusual are the ornaments they've added — that is, the bloodstains in the carpet. "I hope you're not in any criminal databases. I doubt we'll be able to clean all of this up effectively. What did you find?"

"There's a first time for everything," Kian says cheerfully, and, "Knives. Here, look."

He pulls out a loose roll of leather with some silver just visible where it overlaps. With a quick flick of his wrist he lays it flat on the corner of the desk where the body isn't, revealing no fewer than three blades in varying sizes, each with a different mark. One of them seems like the light around it moves strangely, though Rosemary can't quite tell how, and for some several moments she has trouble looking away from it.

Kian doesn't seem to have any trouble, though. "Hmm," he says, thoughtful, and picks that knife up. "Someone's up to something."

"Would you care to elaborate on what, or continue being spitefully mysterious?" Rosemary bites her tongue a moment after — she really doesn't mean to snap. Her patience is stretched thinner than it often is.

"Shall we compromise at 'charmingly mysterious'?" Kian suggests, with another quick flash of a smile.

Rosemary drags her attention away and goes to draw the window shades. They're high enough up, and it's early enough, that observation shouldn't be an issue, but it's something to do, and will contribute to her peace of mind.

"I'll take that as a 'no'," Kian says, a little more dryly. "Mm. I'm not completely certain yet. Fortunately, I don't need to know its purpose to render it inert, and I can do the research later. These symbols are hardly difficult to memorise."

The shades prove to be heavy and dark — blackout shades. Rosemary purses her lips, thinking over the reasons a business advisor would need the accommodation. Frequent migraines, maybe, but she rather suspects something a little more nefarious in this case.

"We won't be able to get — them — out of here, unless you plan to walk them out like Gregory," she says finally, turning. Kian has, in the intervening time, moved back toward Gregory's organs and body, and is doing something complicated with the knife that involves some of his own discarded blood.

"Not a problem," he says absently. "For now, I could use your hands."

Rosemary flexes her hands in response, thinking of the line between killing someone and allowing them to be killed, and then she puts that aside once more and goes to help put Gregory back together.

SEVEN

CONSCRIPTIONS AND CONTRADICTIONS

The most difficult part about putting Gregory back together is determining which knife is safest to use. The one imbued with necromantic power is out: and isn't *that* a fascinating piece of work Kian will need to spend some time investigating? Magically-imbued items aren't unknown, by any means, but they are uncommon, which speaks to either great wealth or great age, or both. Even after bonding it to him, Kian doesn't dare use it for a purpose contrary to what it's meant.

Then, of course, he's obliged to ask Healer Ingram to cut stitches, for no other reason than they're thick enough that doing so himself makes his shoulder burn. He does not have to ask to know the good healer would prefer not to have to heal him a third time; and to her credit she does so without hesitation. Kian had seen the look on her face, earlier — and yet, not a woman given to avoiding pragmatics for shock. His estimation of her rises, a fact he does not intend to mention.

He's never actually asked whether there are side-effects from being healed too often in a short period of time. Perhaps he will ... later.

Kian takes off his glove to handle the organs; it is not the sort he wants sullied if he can help it. The skeleton is limp by then, and the organs falling through ribs and hips, and truly all Kian *needs* to do is ensure they're in the correct places, no connections necessary. ... Or even really possible. The stitches left uncut are just enough to slide organs in without having to be concerned for them falling out once Gregory is upright, given they have no more thread; and with that done Kian scatters a good deal more of his blood into the cavity, murmuring *Folsom Prison Blues* until Gregory shoots upright, gasping for air he only needs in order to speak.

Wincing a little, Kian leans against the bookcase and helpfully holds out the skeleton's scrubs. Gregory snatches them out of his hand with a glare, casting fervent looks at Ingram until she turns around and he can pull some clothes on.

"You're an unmitigated arsehole," Gregory snarls at Kian, to which Kian only smiles brightly.

"I've been told that, yes. When you get to be my age either you stop caring what other people think, or you become someone not worth thinking about. How ever did you die, Gregory?"

"I don't remember," says Gregory sulkily, pulling on the hoodie. "I was around the King's College campus, like I was supposed to be." Trying to find new recruits, no doubt. Kian has stopped trying to tell the church how to work their recruitment drive; if they want to send handsome youngsters to loiter around campuses talking to goths, then he's not going to kill himself banging his head on that particular brick wall.

"Which campus?" Kian asks instead, with a decent presentation of patience.

"The one on the Strand."

As Kian thought. It's about as far to Tower Hill as Tower Hill is from Canary Wharf — though the morgue had been a bit further north. His body must have been picked up in the area. "That woman doesn't look familiar?"

Gregory glances at the assassin and shakes his head. "How *did* I die, anyway?"

"The coroner said you were strangled," Kian answers absently. Strangulation is a violent act, not to mention one which requires strength, which indicates someone larger than Gregory, or at least stronger; and Gregory is skinny but tall. So, more than likely a man. "Do you have a preference for men?"

"What of it?" Gregory demands defensively, and Kian shakes his head with a sigh.

"Gregory, Gregory, Gregory. One does not abandon an assigned mission to go chasing after a pretty face." If he had any blood left, Gregory's face might well be red. As it is he just curses Kian, rather a lot, which Kian proceeds to ignore in favour of limping toward the other corpse in the room. He doesn't attempt to cover the limp: he doesn't have energy to spare, currently, and doing so might only inhibit the layers of healing. Instead he proceeds to do what he ordinarily does first: search the corpse.

"You couldn't have gotten my brain back?" Gregory complains.

"No," Kian answers simply, because he certainly isn't going to explain himself to a rude young cleric with more vanity than sense. A conundrum: the corpse is face-down. Kian considers this difficulty for a moment, considers his shoulder, and before he even has to look up Ingram speaks.

"Can I help?"

"I suppose that's wise," Kian agrees with a straight face. "I'm looking for a phone or a music player."

"All right." She moves closer to go through the corpse's pockets, and Kian wonders whether she's avoiding looking at the assassin's face on purpose or not.

"What about me?" Gregory demands, and Kian turns to him, not bothering to summon sardonic cheer or spite. He's been wounded twice over for this young fool's pieces, and in the end Gregory hadn't even been paying attention while he died. The belief that the dead don't remember is a fancy created by those who only hope their loved ones didn't suffer: Kian has summoned enough deceased to know that traumatic amnesia of any sort has very little to do with memories of the soul. Either Gregory's murderer had been very good between the sheets, or not at all.

"You're dead," he tells Gregory brusquely, "and the only reason you're animated right now is that I can't carry you. My job is to get you back to the church where you can be cremated."

"What!"

For God's sake. "What did you *think* was going to happen?" Kian asks impatiently. "A grand resurrection, an understanding of the meaning of the universe? You're dead. Wherever you go now is the only mystery left to you. Who killed you and why is the mystery left to *me*."

Gregory stares, but at least he's *silent,* and Kian turns back to the corpse and the healer just as Ingram straightens.

"I found this." She holds out a phone which Kian takes. He doesn't even have to turn it over to see if it has a fingerprint scanner: the music player is already on the lockscreen with *Another One Bites the Dust* — that's tritely fitting — front and centre.

"Thank you, Healer Ingram, this is precisely what I need." For her, he can summon cheerful. The situation is hardly her fault, and a little courtesy goes a long way when it comes to those in situations created by others.

"What are you going to do?" she asks, which again is a vindicatingly far cry from a demand.

"First I'm going to restore her soul to see whether she's willing to answer any questions. If she isn't I'll banish her in favour of her corpse so it can get rid of those for us." Kian points at the bloodstains in the carpet.

Ingram nods as if that makes sense. "I didn't realise there was a difference."

"A rather large one, in fact. It is far, far easier to summon a soul than reanimate a corpse alone." If he's lucky, the blade in her brain hasn't interrupted her ability to cast magic. Magical neurology is not, as it were, a highly-researched field of expertise.

Kian uses the blood in his vial for this, and it's a pity he can't gather what he's lost here; it's running low. Still enough for his purposes, even if *Another One Bites the Dust* is not, particularly, the sort of mood music he prefers. The mage stirs, one hand first to push herself upright in a way that would necessitate a groan from the living.

"Bloody hell," she says, sounding more resigned than offended, "somehow one of you lot wasn't on the top of my list."

"What list?" Ingram asks.

"My list of ways I'm gonna die. I always thought necromancers were like goths for magic."

Kian can't help but laugh. This *is* an encouraging start. "Well," he says, "I *am* rather extraordinary, if I do say so myself." Even if the rest of the church have turned into idiots more interested in their catechisms. "You were hired, then."

She nods. "Straight contract job, ongoing, including delivery. You showed up for the organs first."

"What are they for?"

She shrugs. "If I don't ask, I can't tell, and it wasn't offered. Guess that should've been my first clue — you don't tell the hire details when necromancers are involved."

Damn. That means she isn't going to know much at all. Still, she might know *enough*. Kian raises a finger. "Four questions. Who

61

else have you been hired to kill? Who was in the car on Tower Hill Road? What can you tell me about who hired you? Is it the same person who owns this office?"

"I don't know *names*," she says irritably.

"You what," Gregory growls. "You don't even bother asking *names* first? That's just —"

"Gregory," says Ingram calmly, "shut up."

"That was another list," says the assassin. "A necromancer was on it, that's all."

"Then you weren't after Gregory in particular?"

She shakes her head. "I was working with another bloke, no names. He's the one who was in the car, he's the one who picked the necromancer. Gave it my best shot, barely gave me a look, so this other bloke took his best stab. Guess that worked." Wordlessly Gregory grumbles, not quite under his breath. "Think my list was different from his, though."

"Who else was on your list?" Kian asks.

"Earth-sprite fodder —"

"Rude," Kian murmurs, without interrupting.

"— Clairvoyant. Someone with lightning alignment who works in metallurgy."

Kian frowns. "To specify — that wasn't someone in particular? It was the alignment and discipline?"

"Yep. Lightning and metallurgy. Wanted something from each of them, too. Mostly insides."

Then the targets were by magic, not individuals. Interesting, and mildly alarming. One doesn't need such ingredients unless one has a ritual in mind; the only trouble is, Kian doesn't know which, though it's ringing a quiet bell. He indicates the knives still on — or returned to — the leather roll on a corner of the desk. "Do those look familiar at all?"

"Nope."

"And the person who hired you?"

Another shrug. "Intermediaries."

So answers with more questions. Kian shouldn't be surprised, but he will allow himself to be irritated. He's been impaled and then slashed for this. "One last request," he says, and points at the carpet. "I don't suppose you could clean up the evidence for us? I don't particularly care if there's evidence left, as long as it's not *mine*."

"S'pose I can do that," the assassin agrees, eyeing the carpet critically. She reaches out toward the freezer and there's an abrupt gust of ice and cold which makes Gregory yelp and back away. It's a bit like an arctic blast travelling in a straight line across the room, and in moments not only has Kian's blood been frozen beyond help to the modern investigator, but they're all shivering as well.

Well. *He's* shivering. Gregory, of course, no longer feels the cold and Ingram does not seem to mind the cold much, which stands to reason given how her magic feels; Kian hadn't realised light could be quite so chilly. It's just as well, because if she'd been shivering he would have been obliged to give her his coat, and he would prefer not to do that under the circumstances — not the least of which he's going to need it to hide the slash in his shirt.

"Now what?" asks the assassin. "I've never been killed before; I don't know how this works."

"Oh, don't worry," Kian says dryly, while glancing pointedly at Gregory, "that goes around no matter the discipline you're in. Is there someone who'd want to know that you've died? I can give you about an hour to get to them."

"Got a sister out at Ipswich," says the assassin, brightening. "She always said I'd die in a ditch. Won't it be a laugh when I show up on her doorstep instead?"

"Certainly," says Kian cheerfully, shaking some more blood over her head with the easy unspecific measurement one might expect from a chef. "You may as well come downstairs with us, then."

"Thanks for that," she says. "Never knew necromancers could be the decent sort."

"I get that a lot," says Kian dryly as she hops up and pulls her hood up to hide the sticky dampness in her hair and her lack of an eye, to say nothing of the mess on her face.

"No offence on the attempted murder, yeah? It wasn't personal."

"Believe me, if I held grudges against everyone who tried to murder me, I'd have a lot of angry ghosts waiting on the other side." This is not to say that Kian doesn't hold grudges, of course; but it takes rather more than a failed contract killing. He collects his cane and rolls up the knives to stow them in his coat pocket, and glances around while Ingram, shaking her head, goes to close up the freezer.

"Well. Shall we be off before the good Mr Carruthers arrives for the work day?"

EIGHT

TOO-SOLID FLESH

Getting out winds up easier than getting in, even if they're leaving with one more — person — than they went in with. Without Gregory tripping everything up and taking them in circles, getting outside is downright efficient. Of course, the downside to this is that dawn is well underway, light spreading across the sky, and a proper sunrise can't be far behind. Rosemary estimates she's the most reputable of them, and she's carrying an articulated skeleton folded over her arm.

There is no winning. She sets a portion of her focus to plotting an excuse regarding a community theatre production.

Gregory appears to be trying to give Kian the silent treatment, while Kian handles the matter of getting their assassin a train ticket out of London. It's a kind act — kinder than Rosemary had expected. She would say it borders on naïve, if not for the fact Kian had strongly implied he has more years than he looks.

It might border on naïve anyway. Rosemary waits, trying not to twitch at the slowly-increasing drift of passersby. This time of year, people start heading for work before the sun is fully up, but they are largely uninterested, even considering the skeleton. The charms of a big city.

"We'll do with a taxi back to the church," Kian says, once the assassin — or what's left of her — has been handled. He looks at Gregory like he's expecting a flight risk. It might be more reasonable, now that Gregory has his body properly and isn't tripping over too-large boots at every step.

Gregory, arms folded, gives Kian a disdainful look back. Rosemary doesn't rub her temples, because that would be admitting they're getting to her.

"What made you think that wise?" Rosemary asks at length, as Kian moves to the edge of the pavement and scans the street. Even this early, they won't want for a taxi sooner or later, and as long as he's footing the bill, it's practical. "She seemed unusually agreeable. I'll admit I don't know much about necromancy in general; is there some sort of binding to prevent those you call from attacking you or lying to you?"

"Hm?" Kian looks back at her, for a moment disarmed, curious. "No, nothing like that. You haven't met necromancers previously, I take it."

"Well," Rosemary says with a huff. "No actual necromancers, in any case. There is a specific class of people who think *pretending* at necromancy will make for good monetary gains, whether by extortion or faking spiritual connections, but to my knowledge I've never met one of you before in truth."

"Oh, *those*," says Gregory, with a deep sort of disdain. "Only idiots believe in those." He's edging away a little. Rosemary wonders where he thinks he's going to go, if Kian's reanimation has a time limit. What can a man do in one hour?

"The church is perhaps insular," Kian allows, and sets his attention back on the street, lifting an arm to catch the attention of the cab just coming around the next corner.

Privately, Rosemary thinks that there will be a point with an insular, secretive church where they become a cult, but she knows little enough right now that she isn't about to make any wild accusations. More data is required. "Where there is little knowledge, people become afraid," she notes, endeavouring for as flat a voice as possible. No judgment: simply an offering of fact for the necromancers to take into account. "And others use it. Ignorance is a dangerous thing."

The taxi pulls over. "So it is," Kian says, musingly, and the gaze he turns on Rosemary for a moment makes her feel uncomfortably seen. Then it's gone, and the bright inappropriate cheer of him is back. "Well, if you could refrain from quizzing me on *all* the finer points of death-magic in the back of this kind gentleman's vehicle, I think all of our various communities would appreciate it, don't you?"

Rosemary has never been *that* blinded by curiosity, or so she likes to think. "I can wait," she says, with great dignity, and moves to block Gregory's path so that he has no choice but to get into the cab.

Getting into it herself is another adventure entirely, with her skeleton arrayed as gracefully as it can be over her arm. The driver is courteous enough not to eye them too dubiously, only asks after their destination. Rosemary assumes he must have seen far stranger things and far more bodily fluids in his time.

As a consequence of Kian's reminder, the trip passes more or less in quiet, though Rosemary could ask for more comfortable arrangements than the three of them jammed into the back seat, warmth to one side and a preservative-laced chilliness on the other. She wonders a lot of things; but on the whole, without anything immediately occupying and the work of the day catching up, Rosemary mostly starts to yawn.

This would be a terrible place for a nap, especially because if she does doze, she'll likely fall asleep on someone's shoulder. Rosemary turns to her magical awareness instead, comparing the way the men to either side read in her senses. The overall vague feel of them is similar, she decides, an odd sort of low-burning warmth she wouldn't have expected for death mages. The difference is in motion, perhaps. If Kian is a cheerful flame, flickering and dancing from twig to twig, Gregory is a memory of it: cooling ashes, a lingering spark.

The fire metaphor may be wholly unsuitable, but metaphorical accuracy isn't currently on the top of her priority list. Rosemary catalogues the minutia — laments briefly that she cannot get a full assessment of Gregory's state as he is, wearing clothes — and then moves on.

They don't stop quite at the church in question, rather just around the corner — Rosemary feels like it might have been further, as Kian had shifted in his seat and leaned forward a few blocks earlier, but he had eyed her and apparently thought better of it. Unloading is a sight better than loading, as space opens up and Rosemary negotiates her skeleton's wired bones with some care.

"Would you wait here, Healer Ingram?" Kian requests politely, once the matter of paying the driver has been sorted out. "I need to deliver Gregory alone."

Secrets, outsiders unwelcome, or just that it's a sacred space? Rosemary shrugs lightly. "How long will you be?"

Kian considers Gregory. Gregory makes a face. "Not longer than an hour," Kian says after another moment or two. "I'll see you home safely, Healer. Otherwise would be poor thanks. And I haven't forgotten the matter of your invoice, either."

She's not particularly fond of the thought of loitering nearby for an hour, but if all else fails she can likely find a bench or a café within a few blocks. Rosemary nods. "Very well. I'll be nearby, if not in the same precise location." She turns to look at Gregory, who started this whole mess, and purses her lips for a moment, thinking if there's anything to say.

There isn't, really. "Good-bye, Gregory," she says, and moves away to find somewhere comfortable to wait.

The church itself is heavy and stone and fenced, and there's some good space between it and its surroundings; but to the side

Rosemary is on, before too much longer the city picks up again, just as if it had never stopped. She supposes she didn't expect a congregation of necromancers to be somewhere so dreadfully mundane, but as places go, churches tend to develop a sort of weight even if they didn't begin with it. City or no city makes little difference to that.

She paces down the block. There's a bus-stop not too far off, which at least she can sit down at. No one else is there yet — she may move later. For now the skeleton goes across her lap, since it will be difficult to prop on a backless bench, and there Rosemary waits. She passes her time thinking of line items for the invoice she is certainly going to issue Kian, and, after a little while, organising the questions she wants answered about necromancy. There's every chance she can get him to sit down for a little while and bear the questioning once they've returned to the clinic. And then, eventually, when her curiosity is sated, there will be her flat above the clinic, and her own warm bed, and sleep. She already keeps odd hours as it is; what's a few more one way or the other?

Kian comes back less than half an hour later, still limping, still using his cane to decent effect to cope with that problem. Rosemary tilts her head back to look up at him. He hasn't changed his clothes, as she rather thought he might have — he really didn't seem all that pleased with what she provided, like a fastidious cat prevented from shaking tape off its paws — and he's back earlier than he promised. Perhaps he hasn't been staying here, with these local necromancers. But if that's the case, then why?

He stands there for a moment, leaning on his cane, and he doesn't try to loom, which Rosemary appreciates. She gets up, tilts her head at the bag in his off hand. "Surely Gregory wasn't cremated so quickly."

"Hm?" Kian seems bemused for a moment, then makes the connection. "Ah. No. I did, however, think you might appreciate the return of your scarf." He offers the bag to her; Rosemary checks the contents as she takes it, finds not only the scarf she'd lent out but also the clothes Gregory had been wearing.

Everything will need laundering, after the experience with his organs, but it's well enough. "Thank you," she says, letting it settle loosely at her side. "You didn't have any trouble?"

Kian shakes his head. "It's not so unusual a situation as you might think. Most necromancers, of course, aren't murdered at university."

"I imagine most people aren't," Rosemary says dryly, unable to quite resist. Perhaps Kian's sarcasm is catching; perhaps, more likely, she needs to go home and rest.

"You might be surprised," Kian says, measure for measure. Rosemary takes some few moments to decide he's joking. Probably. "Do you wish to be returned to your clinic, or to your home?"

She lifts one shoulder in a half-shrug. "It doesn't matter," she says, and, "I live there." Briefly she wonders if she needs to elaborate that she has a separate space above the clinic, she doesn't make a bed up in her office — no, Kian is likely smart enough to figure that part out for himself, and if he isn't then later Rosemary can either laugh at his expense or tease him, depending.

"Ah." There's no additional comment from Kian, just polite acceptance and realisation. "Then that's where we'll go."

This time, the taxi is far more comfortable. Rosemary handles her skeleton into the middle of the seat, providing a flimsily macabre barrier between her and Kian, and leans forward to give an address. When she sits back Kian has a hand on the skeleton's knee to steady it as they jerk into motion, and his expression is a blandly deadpan sort of thing. One corner of his mouth almost tugs up.

Rosemary doesn't know whether to laugh or take this at face value. She restrains her own potential smile, settles back and eyes Kian across her skeleton's lap.

Kian looks back. "Can I help you with something, Healer Ingram?" he inquires, as if he is completely innocent.

Perhaps he is. Rosemary shakes her head. Now isn't the time for further metaphysical inquiries. "Later," she says, and subsides.

The taxi slows as they get close to home — there's some assortment of emergency vehicles along the streets, and barriers up to redirect some traffic. It's bad enough that Kian has the taxi pull over a block away instead of circling again and again, and as much as Rosemary eyeballs the extra walking on an injured leg with some suspicion, she can admit it's the more practical course of action in this case.

So they approach at Kian's pace, and the smell of smoke hangs in the air and the firemen moving by soot-streaked tell there's been some kind of fire. Rosemary sees a number of disparate facts and can't seem to put them together: first-floor windows blown out at the corner, barriers to prevent passersby sneaking too close to gawk, a hose being stowed, black singe marks up and down the walls thicker as they move along the street, a pair of police officers talking to one of the firemen.

Her clinic's at the corner. How many people will this fire have affected? Surely a number of neighbouring businesses are now going to have to deal with smoke cleaning. Inhalation and subsequent suffocation kill more people, statistically, than the flames themselves, and Rosemary's done her share of treating damaged lungs.

No. Focus. Her clinic's at the corner, and that's important. Rosemary stops when she's stopped by a police officer, professionally brusque. "You can't come this way, miss, they're still looking into the building's stability. It's not safe."

Rosemary looks at the officer, looks at the windows she can clearly see blackened and crumbling shapes through. Looks at Kian, somewhere behind her left shoulder, and finds she can't read his face at all. "... I live there," she says blankly, uncomprehending first because it's impossible to believe, and a few moments later because she doesn't *want* to believe it. Her clinic's at the corner.

The corner of the building is still smoking.

"Miss? We're going to need to ask you a few questions, if you — miss?"

It sounds very distant. "Excuse me a moment," Rosemary says, having to form her words very precisely and carefully. "I think I need to sit down." Her hands are shakier than she's accustomed to. When was the last time she ate, or slept?

She sits on the kerb, for lack of anywhere else, vaguely conscious of Kian's shadow-warmth somewhere nearby and voices over her head. She just ... needs a moment. She'll get back up in a moment.

Nine

A WHIFF OF SMOKE

Healer Ingram does not so much 'sit' as 'sink', and Kian has to wonder how long it's been since she slept. It's been a very full morning even for him; but now, this? It makes no sense.

"Sir, are you able to answer some questions?"

Kian snaps-to with a tightly charming smile. "Of course, Constable. How may I be of assistance?"

Ah, liaising with the non-magical community. How wondrous. He answers questions absently, splitting his attention between looking at the constable's face — he did not hear a name; he does not, at this moment, *care* about a name — and trying to glean as much information as possible from the scene behind the man.

His name is Kian ó Maolomhnaigh (the constable writes 'Molony', to Kian's silent distaste).

No, he doesn't know who could have done this (yet).

Unfortunately, he can't say with surety whether there is anything inside which may have caused it (though he doesn't recall anything which may have done so).

No, he alas does not have Miss Ingram's family details or first name, if you would excuse him, please?

Ingram is trembling on the kerb at their feet. Kian pauses the conversation to pull off his coat and bend — badly — to put it over her shoulders before straightening with a grimace. The constable looks first to his mismatched clothes, and doesn't see where shirt has been cut, covered by waistcoat and made dark by fabric and dried blood.

"It has been an eventful morning," Kian tells him with some degree of genuine weariness, leaning on his cane more heavily than he might be inclined otherwise. Not injured, not *currently*; but opting to make use of it so the constable doesn't attempt to draw things out for too long.

"How's that, sir?"

"For one thing, you may have seen the accident on Tower Hill Road ..."

The constable's gaze sharpens. Kian keeps his tone apologetic. Yes, he was, in fact, involved in that; alas, no, he was rather stunned at the time and didn't think of calling anyone, merely attempting to escape a driver who seemed to have a bad case of enraged fixation ... Not terribly badly injured, no, Constable, but he happened to wander this way ... she was the only one awake and offering assistance ... They left her residence so he could pick someone up and go to his church and she felt compelled to ensure his stability; yes, certainly he has an address.

And so on, and so on. The helpfully well-meaning police are far too good at their jobs for Kian to bother trying to avoid suspicion by refusing to answer: they'd only dig deeply enough to see him as suspicious over time. Best to be open now, and admit to befuddling, and perhaps they'll turn up clues only someone magical can read. Nothing Kian says is much of a lie; he genuinely doesn't know who is behind this.

That, he says with grim focus, glancing past the constable's shoulder. It truly makes *no sense*. Even the ice-mage, killer for hire, had not moved to harm the healer. It isn't a law; the magical community does not precisely have *laws*. It has a set of understandings. There are certain people one simply does not target, not for innocence or incapability, but because they're too important to the cohesion of a society. Not unless those people are the cause of the unravelling, anyway; a healer who betrays their vows is more likely to wind up dead than one who pretends to have skills they don't.

There are few things as important to a lawless society than the value of one's word.

"Are you staying somewhere near here, sir?"

"The Chamberlain," Kian tells him, and motions apologetically down at Ingram. "If I may request your assistance, Constable, having Miss Ingram and I delivered there ...?"

"I'm all right," says Ingram, at first low and rough; and then she clears her throat and gets to her feet, pulling his coat around her with a vague air of surprise that she even has it.

"Do you have anyone we can call, Miss?" asks the constable kindly, and Ingram shakes her head.

"I'll go with — Kian," she says, as if she means for there to be a title or a surname in there and veers away from it in lieu of pronouncing it incorrectly. "What — what happened? If I may ask?"

"We're not sure yet, Miss," says the Constable, "but if you leave your number with me, I'll make sure to follow up at The Chamberlain."

He takes down Ingram's number, and then Kian's as well just in case, and also Kian's room-number, and then waves over one of the officers with instructions to take them to The Chamberlain. It's a short trip, and mercifully one for which Kian does not have to pay; the officer drops them off in front and Kian keeps a close eye on Ingram as they enter. Pale, quiet, both to be expected; no longer trembling, likely not liable toward fainting. But Kian can't be sure, precisely, what's going through her head.

A question to be held in reserve as they come to the front desk. Kian smiles very politely, and requests another room; and when that proves to be impossible on late notice due to popularity, a cot to be set up in his. It is not an elegant solution, but perhaps the better one: if assassins will be coming for them both, better they're in closer vicinity. It might make them easier to find; it will also make them easier to defend.

Of course, there is also the matter of the clothes Gregory had worn, which Kian requests to be laundered, smiling and charming and yes, thank you very much, bring them up to his room when they're done. It's not much in the way of clothes for Healer Ingram, but may be better until something more permanent can be arranged.

When the door is closed and all is silent, Kian turns to Ingram and waits a beat to see whether she intends — or is capable of — saying anything at all. There is a moment when she stares blankly around; and then with an in-drawn breath she turns to him also.

"Why would anyone ...?"

"I don't know," Kian answers simply, the whole truth without smile or gentleness. "Hold that thought, Healer Ingram. I suggest a shower for both of us, with room service and then perhaps some sleep for you."

Her gaze sharpens. "You'll heal much faster if you sleep as well."

"That is likely true," Kian agrees, answering straight-forward for straight-forward, "but at this juncture it would, I think, be unwise for both of us to sleep at once; and, I suspect, I have slept more recently than you. If you would like to set limits on your rest, I shall of course endeavour to wake you on time." He nods toward the wardrobe. "There ought to be dressing-gowns in there. It should do until those clothes are laundered."

He is not, entirely, sure whether he expects Ingram to argue or not; but her gaze follows where he indicates and then, after a moment, she nods, shrugging off his coat to hold it out. "Thank you."

Kian bows and retakes the coat, saying dryly: "It is surely the least I can do at this stage, Healer Ingram."

He can't claim to be entirely responsible; how could he possibly have known that collecting Gregory's remains would lead them to this, or that someone would target a healer of all people? He couldn't. But, even so, the responsibility is partly his if only because the culprit is unlikely to take it themselves. The value of one's word, after all.

Unfortunately it does leave Kian at crossroads until Ingram is done in the shower. He settles for selecting from the wardrobe which of his suits he'd like to wear, and hanging it ready on the back of the bathroom door; and then he clears the desk to unroll the leather in which the knives are contained, to examine the whole package now there's no longer the pressing time-limit of discovery.

That the roll is leather says it's owned by someone older than a half-century: that the edges are woven with style, something potentially silver, says someone with a sense of class: that the weave hides wards says someone with a taste for privacy. The wards are not difficult to circumvent, but it takes a keen eye and a bit of knowledge, of which Kian has both; or at least a sense of obstinacy, which Kian has also. These wards are forget-me-nots, as is the pattern on the edge. Cute.

He doesn't recall wards on the office — nor should there be, if it's intended to be a relatively public place — so both together speaks of someone who enjoys anonymity by obscurity. A wall, after all, declares that there is something to protect. Avoiding notice is in some respects preferable.

The knives, now: the knives are terrifying, in particular that one woven with necromantic discipline. It's far easier to align a weapon than it is to teach it; a dark weapon would have been dangerous enough, but one with this sort of power says the owner is someone old, or at least very well-connected. Disciplining a weapon takes *time*, so at the very least the knife itself is old. There cannot be many soul-reavers about, and Kian will need to return to the church in relatively short order to see whether the archivist has pulled the records for which he asked when he delivered Gregory. The church is supposed to track soul-reavers, or at least their owners; so from where had this one come?

Kian doesn't have much blood left in his jar, but he pours the rest on that knife, murmuring *Let the People Sing* until the knife hears his voice and grudgingly accepts the bond for now. That will stop its owner from scrying it, or trying to use it from a distance; or, at the very least, keep Kian's and Ingram's souls intact and in their bodies while handling the thing. The other two knives aren't as alarming: one Kian recognises as a ritual-cutting knife owing to owning one himself, though likely the ritual is different (and, frankly, it's unnecessary to be so specific; Kian chose his knife for its hilt, heft and blade rather than any other reason). That means there's blood involved in its use, and most likely that of the owner.

Pity blood breaks down so easily. Just knowing it's there means nothing if he can't charm his way into a hospital to have them run a test.

The third is, as far as Kian can tell, lacking in any magical auras at all; but it's made of silver- and copper-wrought glass, and that's inference enough. Of *what*, he can't quite figure; he's no smith or metallurgist. Still, materials are important. The reaver is of bone.

The bathroom door opens and Kian sits back with a breath, considering.

"Have you determined anything?" Ingram asks from the bathroom door.

"Not enough with which to be pleased," Kian murmurs, and rises with a smile and a bow, and examining her past his brow as he does. Her hair seems less luminescent than before, though this could be attributed either to dampness or fatigue and the constant use of energy. She's also less pale than she had been before she sat on the kerbside, but just as drawn. "Room service should be up at any minute."

"Good." Her eyes have ceased being distant; a fact he's obligated to note because she studies him. That, too, is a good sign. "I want to look at your leg and your shoulder before you shower. And I want to know what you intend to do now."

"And whether they may involve my being stabbed or impaled again?" Kian suggests with sardonic humour, which she only answers with a nod. He supposes he can't be surprised by that: so far he's been struck with sharp objects twice in their four-hour acquaintance. "Very well. There are some records at the church I need to secure; that is all the physical exertion I currently anticipate in the near future." Currently. "Other than that, I intend to wait to see what the police have to say when they come to visit."

Ingram's brow furrows. "Why did you tell them about the crash on Tower Hill Road?"

Ah, so she had been listening — even with shock setting in. Kian should not be surprised; a healer of all people should be accustomed to compartmentalisation. Nevertheless, it's a pleasant one. "I've found it easier not to give the police reason to be suspicious by telling them things that are otherwise suspicious in the first instance," Kian says very dryly. "They would surely figure out I was on Tower Hill Road; and then they would want to know why I didn't mention it."

"And Canary Wharf? Won't they figure that out too?"

"They might," Kian admits. "It's entirely possible we were noticed entering and leaving."

"Won't we get in trouble for breaking in?"

Kian smiles. "Oh, Healer Ingram, I only hope so. The only person to get us into trouble is the person whose office we investigated. If our dear Mr Carruthers declares to the police that someone burglarised his office, then we will know who he is."

"And get arrested," she says with some significant exasperation she likely thinks is more hidden than it is.

"This wouldn't be the first time I've had to be sprung from gaol," Kian says dryly.

"I don't have those kinds of resources."

"Nonsense. You have clearly been unexpectedly targeted, or possibly conned by a reprobate cleric — I'm sure the church would be willing to testify as to my degenerate ways. Someone of little criminal record and sincerity as you possess is unlikely to be considered an *accomplice*."

The look she gives him is *clearly* someone trying to be annoyed and failing to hide amusement, and Kian smiles sunnily back, and any impending lecture is promptly curtailed by a knock at the door.

TEN

MELT AND RESOLVE

T hough in theory Rosemary is conscious and present, in retrospect she couldn't say exactly when Kian draped his coat over her shoulders, nor whether any of the things the police have said are actually useful, and certainly not precisely how they managed to get to the hotel. She's ungrounded, loose-drifting, and a strange place free of any familiar things to cause pain can't ground her any more than the familiar made strange by destruction.

Healing is what she knows. The practicalities of healing and doctoring are easy to lean into. She looks sternly at Kian, dredges up half a lecture just in case she needs to convince him of the many values of listening to her — it turns out not to be necessary.

A shower. A shower will help wash off fear-sweat and the lingering scent of smoke, peripheral but no less sharp in her nose for how little she was exposed to it.

This, too, is more or less automatic. She's taken care of herself on less sleep than this when strictly necessary. She notes only vaguely that the bathroom is — very, very nice — and then it's all practicalities again, emptying the contents of her pockets into a neat line on the counter. Phone. Pens. Lint. An old business card of hers.

It's a depressingly small amount to reduce her life to.

Rosemary sheds her clothes and steps into the shower.

The temperature it's set to passes 'warm' and hits 'punishingly hot' within thirty seconds, and Rosemary steps right back out of the shower in a hurry while she tinkers with the temperature, forced now to focus on her surroundings. They must have very good water heaters, which she can appreciate, but she's liable to pass out from heat exhaustion at that rate.

She tests it carefully to make sure it's acceptable before getting back in, and makes a mental note that Kian may have a fascinatingly high heat tolerance, which is forgotten just as soon as soothingly warm water hits her shoulders. Rosemary sighs peacefully, and lets go of a little bit more tension.

Kian's things are in the shower, but so too are the pocket-sized hotel supplies. Rosemary sleepwalks through the mechanics of this, mind drifting back to the clinic. The clinic, and the little flat above it; the place she's spent the last five years making hers. Rowan had been just past ten when they moved in, hadn't nearly started to grow in earnest yet, and the indignity of remaining short far longer than some classmates had led to a neat row of pencil-marks all up one side of the hall.

There's insurance, of course, and still some of the disinheritance bribe tucked away in savings and investments even if most of it had gone to medical school for Rosemary, then, and Rowan's apprenticeship, now. She's not about to be penniless and desperate, though frugality won't go amiss.

But everything she'd built, all the memories tucked into room-corners and odd stains and that one terrible, later-hilarious dent in the wall that truly ensured the security deposit was never coming back — all that is gone, and cannot be reclaimed. The life that was in the place, the things loved and cared for, the particular way the sun filtered through the curtains in the kitchen on summer mornings: all no more.

If Rosemary were of a mood to be optimistic, she might well note that she hasn't been inside yet, hasn't seen what might be saved or what endured. She isn't. Better to assume the loss now, and weather it, rather than expect hope to carry her through.

At least there are the photos she had the foresight to save digitally, but she doesn't even have a charger for her phone, for pity's sake. Rosemary is laughing before she can help herself, something hysterical and half-choked, and as she hunkers down to get hold of herself tears take over, shaking her whole body with the force of feeling. She leans into the tile at the side, solid and cool and resolute, and there she stays for a long, long time.

The water is starting to cool noticeably even to her by the time she rouses herself, rinses the last of conditioner from her hair and shuts off the shower. By some mercy Kian hasn't knocked at the door — either she hasn't been very long in truth, or he's occupied and giving her the space to exist unobserved, which she finds she owes him a profound gratitude for.

She dries off slow and methodical, puts on the dressing-gown she vaguely remembers retrieving earlier. It's of terribly good quality, and the feel is pleasant enough, but she's going to want for things like undergarments before very long.

A sleeve swiped across the mirror clears enough of it to get a quick look at herself. She hasn't gone too blotchy with crying, and the heat-flush will fade soon enough — no one should be able to tell she's been having significant emotions, let alone weeping fit to burst. Good. She does seem to recall Kian said something about room service, now that she's thinking about it.

All the same, leaving the bathroom does require some amount of steeling herself.

But it's easier than she thought it would be, to slip into standard patterns, once she's faced with Kian again. He's clearly been studying, and if there's one thing Rosemary knows, it is the refusal of the independent-minded to rest easily. Ask and answer, lecture and frown, and — oh, spirits help her, the man's sense of humour is growing on her.

That is definitely the stress of the day talking. Rosemary is *not* reassured by how Kian speaks so easily of fobbing the blame for the last several hours off on him, even if the break-in definitely is his responsibility. 'Reprobate cleric' about sums it up, and she's about to tell him as much when there's a knock at the door.

She flinches, heart jumping with a sudden alarm she thoroughly detests, and turns on the spot to eye the door. That must be the promised room service. Only — what if —?

"I'll handle it," Kian says easily, and Rosemary can't even bring herself to argue for the sake of the injury she means to look at. She nods instead, slips past him to the desk with the knives laid out and links her hands behind her back so she won't be tempted to touch.

Kian answers the door. Rosemary, staring at a knife, hears only the low murmur of conversation, nothing distinct. She's sick of this already and it hasn't even been a full day. Whoever torched her clinic isn't playing by any set of rules she knows, and that's putting her on shaky ground in an entirely different way from her sudden rootlessness.

And she hates being afraid and adrift. She hated it when she was sixteen and freshly disowned; she hates it now, back at square one.

How *dare* they.

By the time Kian has balanced the tray of food on the table that isn't full of knives, Rosemary has settled herself, if not with calm then with a low-burning anger. "I certainly hope you got extra," she says, turning back toward him as blandly business-like as she knows how.

"Would I ignore a healer's recommendation?" Kian inquires in his sweet-sarcastic way.

"Yes," Rosemary says, though it doesn't come out quite as sharply as she had intended it to.

Kian raises an eyebrow at her, after a moment bows his head in mock concession. "At my own peril, surely," he says. "There is more than enough, and certainly better than earlier fare."

Rosemary is not going to agree to this until she's tested it. "Where were we?" she says instead, drawing herself back to the topic at hand.

"Canary Wharf and your spotless record," Kian says. "Please, go ahead." This with a gesture at the food. "We're not in an immediate rush, I think. It will be a little harder for someone to burn down The Chamberlain unnoticed."

It stings, unexpectedly. Rosemary frowns at him and goes to take a seat. She isn't particular about food specifics, pays more attention to portion sizes and distribution of proteins than anything else. "You said you were waiting on the police, and there are records from your church that may help," she says as she selects, recapping to ensure it sticks in her mind. "What of the knives?"

"As I said, not enough to be pleased with — hence the check of records." Kian sits at ninety degrees from her, decorous despite the degradation of his suit. "I've learned a little from them, but more ... observations of character, shall we say, than anything like material evidence." He graciously chooses from what Rosemary's set apart from her, doesn't quibble about any of the decisions made; and more than that he's watching her, studying in a way that unsettles only because Rosemary finds she isn't quite sure what he's looking for.

Rosemary eyeballs him in return for a moment, and then turns her attention to eating, herself thinking through the chains of events. The theft of Gregory's body; the assassination attempts twice on Kian; the arson of her clinic. Something isn't fitting quite right among those, but the whole thing is surreal and peculiar enough it might be anything. She'll have to sleep on it.

"If you preferred it," Kian finally says, carefully, "it might be safest for you to leave the country for a little while. If you hadn't considered the option. Between Gregory and the knives, it seems fairly clear this is an issue of necromancers for the most part, into which I have inadvertently dragged you."

She hadn't even considered it, now that he mentions it. Granted, her thinking hadn't progressed all that far beyond shock in the first place. She could join Rowan in France — perhaps see if the French she remembers is good enough for the libraries there —

It's a nice fantasy for the space of about twenty seconds, before the angry coal-burn seeps through it. Rosemary shakes her head. "You're still my patient, and I want answers. For all of this. Since you don't have them, I'll take them from whoever does."

Kian pauses another moment, then inclines his head to her in turn. "Well said, Healer Ingram," he says, and there's some note of approval in his voice that she doesn't think she's imagining. Well, fair enough; she's more or less just declared her intention to help with his problem in the long term, anyway.

He doesn't add anything more for the moment, and the silence of eating turns companionable. Rosemary debates over pressing Kian for whatever details he *did* turn up in his study of the knives, but now that she's sitting and approaching resting, she can feel how tired she is. It's a sort of sinking-in exhaustion, heavier and heavier with time, which means new information is going to be harder to retain. Pressing him for full information in the morning will be better than now. Morning, or whenever she wakes up.

After this much work, it might well be morning again. First things first. Rosemary eats more or less automatically, lays utensils down neatly, and rises when she's done in short order. Kian's being rather more leisurely about things, and if he's eating while she heals she'll have to track *those* biological processes. She'd prefer not. Rosemary resorts to pacing along the length of the bed and back again while he finishes.

She's genuinely not trying to rush him, only to stretch her legs and keep herself alert until she can look at him, but when Kian puts his fork down he doesn't look like he's quite finished.

"I believe you said you wished to take a look at my injuries before bed?" he offers.

Rosemary doesn't customarily experience embarrassment in volumes large enough to cause any physiological reaction, but she can feel her scalp tingling with some involuntary circulation of vital energy anyway. "So I did," she says, striving to reclaim her usual sense of dignity. "I don't think it will be for the best to push your body further right now, but I want to at least check that you haven't re-opened anything."

Kian nudges his chair back from the table to offer her room. "Where do you want me?" Rosemary hesitates, briefly and terribly aware of the setting, of the fact the vast majority of her patients have been seen in an office or operating-room and this is a very well-appointed suite.

— It's nonsense. She's over-tired. If she has energy to worry about social implications of being alone with a well-formed man, she has energy to heal. Brisk, chin tilted up, Rosemary crosses the distance between them. "Here is fine," she says, and leans over to get hands on him.

There's still a cut in his shirt over the shoulder wound, which means she doesn't need to undress him to get at it. She plucks the fabric apart a little, assesses visually first — all well enough, for a fresh barely-closed wound, no atypical swelling or discharge — and then sets her fingers to his skin.

He's a little chilly. Perhaps it's the differential — she's been in a hot shower recently enough, after all. Rosemary closes her eyes and focuses on the workings of his body. Circulation as it should be, temperature ... a little low, perhaps, but not attributable to anything on an immediate scan. It's possible he's just lost a little too much blood today, which will be fixed with time and hydration.

It's a little bit of a stretch to focus on the thigh wound from here, but Rosemary can do it, and frankly, she doesn't feel like dealing with the pants situation. She's aware her balance is suffering a little, but she leans on Kian and proceeds.

The thigh, as it's been walked on, has a number of little stresses. Nothing's broken open again, none of her work is entirely undone, but it hasn't progressed as much as she'd like for the amount of energy fed to it, either. Rosemary hums a mildly disapproving note, but doesn't fuss with it yet, instead stands back and lets go. "You're fine for now," she says, opening her eyes. "Be careful of them in the shower, and once you're out I don't want you walking for as long as is possible. When I wake up again, I'll see about another round."

His brows go up. "Is this generosity or practicality, Healer Ingram?"

"Practicality," Rosemary says. She entertains a brief fleeting fantasy of the invoice she'll deliver to him later. "The sooner you're entirely back together, the sooner you'll stop damaging it while you're healing, and as someone has now tried to kill you *twice*, I would not assume it will be the last time in the immediate future."

"A logical concern, at this point," Kian agrees. "Very well. I shall ... do my best to stay off of it."

Rosemary eyes him dubiously, since it's not a promise — but she supposes she couldn't hope to ask for one at this point, not with the future uncertain. It will do. "Thank you," she says, and while he finishes the remainder of the food, she turns her back on him and eyes the bed. There was mention of a cot, she recalls, but it hasn't made an appearance yet — perhaps because the staff assumed no one would immediately need a cot at whatever hour of the morning this is. Hm.

"Wake me if you intend to sleep," she directs, reasoning that this will cover the disposition of sleeping surfaces, and topples into bed, asleep before she has the presence of mind to navigate blankets.

ELEVEN

A BRIEF PAUSE

K ian has no intention of waking Ingram when the cot arrives — which it does in short order, after Kian has finished with his meal and most likely perfectly timed so the food trolley can be removed in the same trip. In light of weariness and injuries, he allows them to make the cot themselves; it's hardly even qualified to be called a *cot* — that is, being *over*qualified.

Only once there's no others in his room does he rise and go to pull down the covers on the side Ingram had not fallen over, and then go around to pick her up and bring her around so she can be under the covers. She's lighter than he expects, and shorter than he remembers — or at least seems so held like this. In moments he has her securely in bed, covers drawn up and tucked in. No point in her catching cold for sleeping on top of the covers.

Then it's his turn for a shower, as careful as he knows how to be with barely-closed injuries. The water at first feels shockingly cold, and even after turning the knob it doesn't warm up all that much; and it takes a shivering moment before Kian recalls how long Ingram had had the shower running and the likelihood of there not being hot water afterward.

Fine. He'll just have to suffer tepid water, though it means he emerges feeling distinctly grumpy. He rather dislikes too-cold showers.

At least, finally, he can dress in a matching suit instead of those horrid track-pants; and now he feels somewhat human again. He leaves off the coats while in the room, and doesn't bother with shoes for the same reason, and instead sits down again at the desk, considering the knives, and then the skeleton sat in the corner, and then the cot. Sleep is really something he ought to be doing; but the thought of both of them asleep, after a twice-attempted murder and successful arson, does not fill Kian with confidence. But they do still have the skeleton, which Kian might be able to animate even without a soul ... perhaps. The effort ratio may not be good enough, if it's only for peace of mind.

The phone ringing solves the issue, and Ingram doesn't even stir; when Kian answers it's reception calling to let him know a constable has arrived to meet them, which is certainly prompt of them. Then again, it's been at least a couple of hours, judging by Kian's pocketwatch; and he is not all too surprised they may wish to follow up. Particularly if anyone *has* reported a break-in at Canary Wharf. Things could get dicey if that's already occurred, as Kian isn't entirely sure Ingram would even wake up for it.

When the constable knocks on the door Kian answers with a smile which is rather easier to pull on than it had been a couple of hours ago, and yet still isn't entirely up to snuff. It'll do, for the circumstance, and he takes no offence when there is no such response from the constable.

"Come in, Constable," Kian says cheerfully, pointing toward the armchairs and tapping his mouth with a finger. "Quietly, however; Miss Ingram is asleep and though I doubt a herd of elephants could wake her, best not test that theory."

He can see the gaze around, the way the constable's eyes clock the cot, and the lump that is Ingram. This, as much as comfort, is why Kian had spared the time to tuck her in: he assumes it's better than anyone seeing her in a bathrobe, regardless of how thick or fluffy.

Kian does not attempt to hide a limp, once more, as he takes a seat in the armchair left and reclines, arms resting. It's not his, but he's been staying here for weeks already, so it may as well be. "How can I help you today, Constable?"

With not much, it seems, which is both a relief and an irritant. There have been no apparent reports from Canary Wharf; Kian almost would have preferred that there had been, if only to advance the investigation and take advantage of the church's coffers when they have to pay his fine. Petty, perhaps, but everyone must have some petty vices.

No. Mostly the constable wants to ask about the car on Tower Hill Road, and how he met Ingram, and a myriad of small details for which Kian has nothing but honest answers and thinly-veiled obfuscation. The difficult ones involve 'Why did you go to the church before reporting to the police?', to which Kian leans heavily on doctrine and speaking of theological matters obscure enough to make eyes glaze over. The police have, it seems, already visited the church; and this Kian expected, and indeed relied upon, for the church is nothing if not predictable.

Predictable in throwing the reprobate Irishman under the bus, that is. Turning this into an international incident throws a wrench in the constable's ability to investigate Kian, to which Kian can only shrug apologetically. He hadn't, he says charmingly, thought that he was a suspect.

They investigate everyone, naturally. Of course they do. But there's nothing to suspect, really, as it's plain that Kian had been with Ingram and therefore couldn't have burned down her clinic.

(No; he suspects it's a matter of the car and the assumed attack, and the suspicion that Kian might have dragged someone innocent into some kind of illegal and violent activity. As Kian truly does not know who's behind the attack, there isn't much he can say that makes him culpable for anything: at least not until the constable asks why he caught a taxi back from Canary Wharf.)

Too good for secrecy, that's for sure.

He was tracking down a wayward young cleric, Kian explains. He'd been on a university campus, then went elsewhere without reporting in ... He returned the young reprobate to the church, though honestly, the way young people are trained these days, he can't speak all that much to what he may have been doing at the Wharf ... Please, Constable, feel free to speak to the church on the matter.

This is, potentially, dangerous: the church in England does not particularly like Kian; but then, even the church in Ireland doesn't particularly like Kian, which is why they sent him over here. He's a liaison: pushing that back on this church's native ambassadors could backfire spectacularly on him personally. It could also make him look better to the police, if the church stonewalls the constable as much as Kian assumes they will.

In the end there's only a few things of worth to discover out of the interview: Kian's assessment of Mr Carruthers's age should run to the high side, which means there's only a handful of disciplines he can possibly possess. Someone younger would have cast their lot to the police: only those too old and full of themselves would overlook them. Even most mages, unless specifically a magical issue, use the police. Nothing else makes sense; there is no universal governing body for the disparate magical communities in the British Isles, given their size. Some on the continents have some degree of oversight; others, like elfin societies, have their own and don't ordinarily interact outside their borders.

Kian closes the door on the constable with a frown, drumming his fingers. This does make things a touch easier, but in the most irksome manner. Old and with a soul-reaver narrows the field — but it means returning to the church, who are already annoyed with him, and will shortly be more so owing to the fact that Kian has thrown them under the bus. Perhaps he should try to get there first.

He glances once more at the lump under the covers that is Ingram, and then goes to the skeleton, pulling it up to sit it in the armchair like a macabre guest. He cannot, truly, afford to shed more blood tonight; so he goes instead to get the soul-reaver, using it to nick the base of the skull while murmuring *Let the People Sing*. The knife vibrates, at first grudgingly and then livelier, and the skeleton's fingers twitch, and reach for the knife. Kian lets it take it, and the last thing he does before he leaves is to call downstairs to request a cab and that no one, under any circumstance, comes into his room. There. That takes care of potential collateral damage.

Coats and shoes on, cane in hand, and at the door Kian glances back at the skeleton in the armchair. It sits, grinning, with knife in hand and an eerie glow in its eyes that makes it seem as if it's meeting his gaze. Even necromancers can feel chills.

Kian suspects that he might, after all this is done, realise just how reckless he's been with that weapon in his ignorance, and shiver. For now he leaves with the uneasy feeling like he's left a dragon guarding Ingram thinking it's a puppy, and goes downstairs. The cab is already waiting, and the church is not far: though further than it was by time, now there's traffic on the roads. Still better than over-working his thigh; he promised, after all, he would attempt to stay off it.

The church is typical of London: old, small but of a style which harks to cathedrals and grandeur, full of stained-glass and with hymnals sounding on the weekends. Mostly dirges; the church is not known for being cheerful, more's the pity. There's something of a yard, and a billboard at the front, and a nicely winding path to the door: and nothing at all, really, to indicate that it isn't a normal non-denominational church. Of course, if one went there on a Sunday the rituals and liturgies would be rather different, which is why it only advertises closed services — and if one has to ask,

101

one isn't on the list. Kian, however, is, and therefore strolls right in, leaning on his cane, and knocks on the door.

It opens and the doorkeeper looks out, and Kian smiles sunnily, and the door closes again with a thud and an 'ugh'.

"So delighted I'm so welcomed at the house of our faith," Kian murmurs, and the door opens again.

"You're bringing trouble to the house of our faith," snaps the doorkeeper, but she stands grudgingly aside.

"Dear Gregory did that," Kian answers, a little less cheerfully, and steps in, moving past her toward the back of the church. The block is just large enough to touch the apartments behind, owned also by the church; which is a damn sight better than being underground, as Kian has heard some enclaves do. Or totally underground, at least, since the church extends in both directions. Kian moves to the back of the church past the hall, where the kitchen and storage are, and an extra door which seems like it might be more storage; it leads directly into the back of the apartments through the fence.

The wards don't deny him as he enters more properly, though the secondary doorkeeper here looks likewise unhappy to see him. She says nothing, he smiles at her anyway, and continues on his way.

Usually one might expect the higher ranks to be at the top; the church's priorities are rather reversed, with the senior clerics underground. The library is on the first floor, easily accessible to most and without the risk of mildew inherent in basements; on the ground floor are such boring things as amenities and the guest-rooms of which Kian did not partake (and frankly nor do many others). It's the library he wants, at any rate, and coming up from below means he doesn't have to fight the initiates using the library for their studies. Frankly, the library is the most compelling place here.

Made of the entirety of the floor and with windows heavily shaded against the day's sun, it's one of the best libraries in England, albeit one most people can't conceive exists. From the outside the building looks ramshackle and old-world; on the inside it's buttressed with wards and walls, lights through slits and on lanterns converted to electrical power for safety as well as aesthetic. Kian wanders between the bookcases, footsteps and cane-end soft on the runners, quietly observing studying acolytes while meandering in the direction of the head archivist's office. They do seem earnest; it's delightful to see, for all Kian's irk at Gregory. One young cleric does not a demographic make, and handsome young men can be an arrogant lot. He should know; he was one.

The archivist's door is open, as it has been every time Kian has visited. Kian raps the head of his cane against the jamb and enters without needing to sidle. The stacks of books and papers are not approaching lethal, though Kian has to wonder what's in there which isn't important enough to be cared-for properly, and yet is worth keeping.

"I'm in here," Archivist Albinson says from around a corner of a bookcase, and when Kian puts his head around she looks up, her eyes frowning and her mouth smiling. "Oh, it's you. Do you have the soul-reaver?"

This, Kian reflects, is why one cannot underestimate the cerebral. "Not on me," he says. "Did you find something, or was I merely too obvious?"

"You asked me who has soul-reavers. What else could it be?"

"A murder."

She waves a hand, turning to rifle through a stack of clean white printouts. "I hear Gregory was complete enough to start crying before your bond ran out. I don't know what they're teaching new clerics these days."

At least there's *one* person to like here, Kian decides. "You're in a prime position to correct them, I'm sure. Are those the records in question?"

"That's right." She brings them over to put them down on the side-table enclosing the corner, at right angles to the bookcase and with a gap for egress. There are an alarming number of them, given the subject. "Can you narrow it down any further?"

"He's in one of the immortal disciplines, so if it's inherited it's unlikely to be recent."

"Ah; that *does* narrow it down. I assume not a necromancer."

"Doubtful," Kian agrees with a straight face, but that is immediately put on his list of things to do: investigate ties between the office and the church. He knows a technomancer with a talent for tracking money; she's in Ireland, but the distance is hardly a deterrent these days. It's unlikely he'll get anywhere with that, but it's worth ruling out. Necromancers are among the most numerous of the immortal disciplines, to say nothing of the most solitary. "But I can take all of those, nevertheless. Leaving no stone unturned, and all that."

She looks a little disappointed by that, and promptly scowls and shoves the pages at him. "Fine. See if I put in the extra effort."

Kian takes them and bows. "Archivist Albinson, I assure you, you currently hold the highest competence in the London Church in my esteem. If I require any research expertise, rest assured I will come to you."

Her feathers smoothed, she calms down and turns, waving him off; and Kian turns to head out of the church, tucking the papers away in the inside pocket of his coat.

Twelve

MAKE NO BONES

It isn't light or magic or violence that wakes Rosemary finally, but sound. Kian's voice, in tones that are shading away from sarcastic and somewhere toward genuinely annoyed. At least, that's her best judgment from having known him maybe twenty-four hours and having been awake only half of that.

She doesn't move or open her eyes immediately, instead waits and assesses. There's a weight over her, and she's warm even though she would swear she passed out on top of the covers. Almost too warm. There's no unusual quality in the light through her eyelids, and in fact there's very little of it at all, so more than likely a lamp or nothing is on.

Kian sounds like he's arguing.

"Give that to me," he says, a little more sharply. "It isn't yours."

Rosemary waits for a response, hoping to learn something of Kian and the unexpected guest from this, but no response follows. Instead, there's only Kian again.

"Putting it into your hands constituted a loan," Kian says, still sharp-exasperated. "That purpose has been served; you have fulfilled your duty. Return the blade to me, please."

At least he's polite about it — more or less. Perhaps he's on the phone, but it's quiet enough Rosemary rather thinks she'd hear at least some piece of sound from the other end of the conversation, even if not intelligible words.

"No, I'm not going to play tug-of-war with you for it."

Someone in the room, then. Someone so quiet they can't be heard to pace or shift or breathe, someone who will not or cannot speak —

Rosemary puts these facts together to a conclusion she immediately dislikes. She's alarmed enough by the possibility that she sits up rapidly, shedding blankets.

Kian turns his head toward her. So, too, does the skeleton he's arguing with. There's an odd glow flickering deep within the skull, leering out the eye-sockets and nasal cavity. Rosemary is unsurprised, but disappointed, to observe that the skeleton is holding one of the knives Kian had been studying.

"Healer Ingram," Kian says brightly, as though he is not arguing with an animated skeleton over a potential murder weapon. "Good evening."

"Is it?" Rosemary inquires. The curtains are drawn, after all, and between the deep sleep she's had and the shock she — isn't thinking about at the moment — she has rather misplaced her sense of time.

"Perhaps a little further on to night," Kian allows, and looks back at the skeleton. "*Now* will you give me the knife?"

The skeleton backs away and sits down in the armchair. It's a remarkable display of coordination for a creature held together with wire — and in some places not even that. Kian watches it with his mouth at an unusual disapproving slant. He's not quite so far gone as to fold his arms, but Rosemary would be able to tell even without the half-verbal argument that things have not, precisely, gone to plan.

"You said something earlier about your animations not necessarily being bound to listen to you," she says wryly. Carefully she swings her feet out of bed and to the floor, checking her own status. A little sore — but a general aching malaise, not anything specific, save the slight rawness in her palms and knees from having been shoved to the floor earlier. Nothing that requires individual addressing at the time. She straightens her dressing-gown, checks that it's not going to do anything embarrassing, and gets up.

"I did, didn't I," Kian agrees, amiably annoyed. "Yes. They don't need to tell me the truth, they're not bound to follow my orders. Anything I animate listens to my requests thanks to a sense of obligation or hope, and they tend to be more agreeable when they lack a brain or when what I ask aligns with their desires anyway. They are free to flee from me or even attack me — although it would be terribly gauche."

Somehow, a day ago, Rosemary would have imagined true necromancy to be a great deal more commanding, all corpses and binding commands rather than negotiations and reuniting organs with torsos. Now, of course, she has met Gregory and all of his opinions.

"Shouldn't your animation run out after a while?" she inquires next, lifting her chin toward the skeleton now simply watching them.

"Yes," Kian says crossly. "It should."

They consider that in a silence flavoured with concern. Rosemary can't bring herself to be outright alarmed just yet, when so far the worst the skeleton has done is refuse to give Kian the knife. "Have you slept at all?" she asks, eying his clothes. He's fully dressed, so either he's slept and gotten up again in the interim, or he hasn't slept.

Kian nods distractedly. "There's no need to fret for my well-being, Healer Ingram. I've slept well enough, and I've been cautious with my leg."

This immediately makes Rosemary suspicious. She looks over the room again for changes that might have occurred while she was unconscious, other than the blankets that someone — likely Kian, now that she thinks of it — had drawn over her. There's a cot, of course, or something a little fancier than, with linens mussed enough to have been slept in; on the table at the other end of the room there's a careful stack of file-folders, which she is reasonably sure were not there when she went to sleep.

Either someone has visited, or Kian has gone out.

Rosemary lines up the facts and makes an educated guess. "You animated the skeleton to keep watch, because you left to retrieve those files." It would be why he volunteered that he was cautious with his injury, when if he had simply *rested* there would be no need to be cautious, because he wouldn't have been doing anything ill-advised in the first place.

Kian hesitates briefly, taking his gaze from the skeleton to glance back at her once more; Rosemary does her best to look as though she knows exactly what he did, although she is, in fact, at least half bluffing.

After another moment or two Kian shakes his head. "I suppose there's no point in hiding it, unless I can thereby escape the lecture regarding proper after-care ...?"

Rosemary reminds herself not to be endeared. She moves toward the table with the files, careful to move around Kian rather than crossing between him and the skeleton. *Her* skeleton, she is rather reminded. It may never be the same. "You must realise I lecture out of a sense of concern rather than moral superiority," she says stiffly, and leans over to look at what he's brought back. "If you're determined to damage yourself, there's little I can do. What's in these?"

"Information," Kian says, demonstrating helpfulness that any cable company would surely admire. "I hardly enjoy potentially causing myself irreparable damage, Healer Ingram. Acquiring these was time-sensitive; I deemed the risk necessary and acceptable, in light of that."

"What type of information?" Rosemary is already opening the top file to get some sense for what it is, and Kian hasn't moved to stop her though surely he could, so she judges that a sort of acquiescence. The top sheet tracks a family lineage, with names that look to Rosemary to be primarily Italian. It's ... not what she expected. Further papers in that file have sketched thumbnail-portraits of an assortment of people who broadly resemble each other, as well as a more detailed sketch of a long knife. It bears some resemblance to the one the skeleton holds now, though in markings more than shape. "Ah. The knife?"

"The knife," Kian says. His stare-off with the skeleton is going nowhere. "It's a type of specific and rare necromantic artifact, which takes a great deal of effort to make. These files are records of people and families who are known to have made or possessed one at any point in the last thousand years or so."

"That's rather a broad span," Rosemary says absently, and then considers the size of the stack. For a thousand years of records, this is actually fairly slim.

"I don't intend to let anything slip through the cracks," Kian says grimly. He steps back, still watching the skeleton, and finally sighs and turns his head away. "Well, that's going to make comparing any records rather annoying, but it seems to be content to stay as-is for now."

Rosemary eyes him. She has a number of questions and the distinct feeling that asking too many at once is going to result in frustration. "You're very calm about this."

"Becoming angry with it isn't going to help anything," he says. His tone is already sliding back toward his customary light-edged cheeriness. "Either it will give up eventually, or it won't. For now, I can focus on this *and* observe its actions."

She shrugs, a little uncomfortably, and separates his stack of files in half, moving the bottom set toward him as Kian comes over to take a seat. He limps exaggeratedly as he goes, making a show of putting little to no weight on the injured leg. Rosemary has no doubt this is an annoyance for her benefit, and as a consequence completely ignores it.

"Are these comprehensive?" she asks as she sits in turn. "That is, will we need to visit other churches for records that span other locales?" The chair is a little too big to be comfortable, but she doesn't want to risk tucking her feet up while still stuck in only a dressing-gown. The whereabouts of her previous and currently only clothes are unknown at the moment, however. Rosemary resigns herself, blowing the frustration out in a short puff of a sigh before focusing down on the files before her.

The knife sketched in the Italian family's folder isn't a close enough match for the one in the skeleton's hand. Rosemary closes that file, sets it to her left, and opens the next.

"There might be one or two they've missed, but those would be outliers." Kian flips through several papers of portraits, hums idly as he pauses over text. "There was an archival digitising effort some years ago. Some senior clerics were convinced to see the value of off-site backups."

It's such kindly bland phrasing that Rosemary almost doesn't have to think of what kind of inciting incident might cause such a shift in opinion. Almost. Fires are a terribly well-known bane of the preserved and the archived. She grimaces, looks down at what she has. This file is even more scant than the previous one: it pins a small, jagged blade with a distinctive hilt and the appropriate markings as being located somewhere in the Appalachian Mountains. Probably.

Not their target. This one, too, Rosemary sets aside.

"What *is* the magic on this blade?" she wonders aloud, some few files further into the effort.

It's only because she's lifted her eyes briefly that she catches Kian's grimace. "It's a necromantic magic," he says, "but not as you would think. So far as I can tell, it prevents a soul from being recalled to the body it is used on."

"So far as you can tell?" Rosemary lifts her tone just enough to make it a question. This next file might be promising, but it's a scan of a *very* old document, and one not written in English; there are translations in a firm, blocky hand on a second sheet. The translator doesn't seem to have heard of lowercase letters.

"I haven't seen one in person before," Kian says. "There's something strange about it. I might be able to ascertain further details if I was allowed to study it again —" This is accompanied by a pointed look at the skeleton still holding the knife and appearing to observe.

The skeleton takes no note of the pointed look.

"— that may be some time away." Kian bends his head over his current set of papers again.

Rosemary isn't sure she quite has the significance of soul versus body-only animation, but she's too distracted by trying to extract the most meaningful parts of this translated journal to ask right at the moment.

The one she has at hand really does look promising. Rosemary sets it to her right once she's established this, and then keeps going. They pass the time this way, with fewer questions between them, and Rosemary finds she rather approves of the way the silence is broken only by Kian's intermittent humming and the shift of papers against each other. She isn't much of one for music, but he has a nice enough voice and it's a good sight better than *complete* silence.

When she comes to the end of her stack, it's only the one with the old journal translation that has looked as though it might be relevant. It's a precious little result for what's ostensibly a thousand years' worth of records. Rosemary flips it open again, squints at the tiny thumbnail-sketch of a blade.

Someone who had studied light would be able to bend the light itself to magnify the sketch. Rosemary's alignment hums under her skin, reminding her of the shapes she's bent it into, and the things she's avoided. With a sigh Rosemary gets up, that sheet in hand, and moves closer to the skeleton, cautious.

Its head turns to watch her.

"Can you please hold up the knife?" Rosemary asks. Perhaps if she doesn't ask it to give her the thing, only show it to her. "I'd like to make a comparison."

The skull tilts. The lights inside it flicker. The knife comes up, held horizontal.

"... Interesting," Kian says softly somewhere behind her.

Rosemary doesn't waste time, holds up the page and runs a quick visual comparison. It's small, but it's the best match she's seen yet, and there are only so many shapes blades come in, aren't there?

She'd prefer not to be near the skeleton any longer than she has to be. "I appreciate it," she says, recalling her manners, and backs away to show Kian what she's found.

Thirteen

THE VAGUEST TRAILS

O f the entire stack, it proves that only two are alike enough
to be their weapon: and of those, only Ingram's has
an image of any kind. They exchange and compare, and Kian
frowns thoughtfully as he reads the journal entry Ingram found.
"Interesting," he murmurs. "Looks like it came from Europe. This
is quite an old record, however; thirteen seventy-six."

"Do you know the writer?"

"Necromancers often spend their first couple of centuries
in their own countries," Kian answers absently, tapping the
signature. "It's not a name I recognise offhand, but that doesn't
mean they're dead, or indeed haven't written anything else.
Itinerant necromancers keep copious journals." This suggests
another trip to the church; Kian would like to avoid that, if
possible. By now surely the police have gone back. Perhaps he

should simply call this time ... at least something emailed is readable.

He holds out his hand for the page he'd found, and studies them side-by-side for a moment. A pretty redhead from Finland ... a handsome brunette in Prague. There is a good few centuries between them, and when Kian briefly calculates travel speed, he estimates the knife could, indeed, be on the British Isles. And yet: someone would have had to bring it here. Someone not either the man from Finland or the woman in Prague.

"Did you find something?"

Ingram's question makes Kian realise his frown has deepened, and he consciously smooths his face, and straightens. "After a fashion," he murmurs, "if one counts the *lack* of it to be 'something'. This blade has changed hands at least twice in the last few centuries: and yet, we have no record of the owners, or what happened to them; only that they wound up dead. This is ... quite concerning. These people have gone to great lengths to avoid being discovered; which tallies rather well with my observations of Mr Carruthers thus far."

He reaches for his phone to take a picture of the two pages together, and sends it to the archivist requesting any further records by the authors.

"What now?" Ingram's tone is business-like rather than questioning, which Kian appreciates. He is most frequently obliged to face these situations alone. There is a difference between consulting an equal and caring for a dependent.

"We have a few options ahead, in truth," Kian admits. "The archivist at the church seems intrigued, and I daresay she will become alarmed at the idea we have so few records and no names." This may come back to bite him, if she tells the other clerics, but such a discrepancy in the church's records is not a situation only for the English Church to handle. No, he believes he can make some deals there: he may not be liked for his methods, but those methods are why he's been given the position he has. His people don't like him; they don't dare refuse him. "The other options involve investigating the others on the assassin's list: an earth-intent mage, a clairvoyant, and someone with a lightning alignment in metallurgy."

"Earth-intent mages aren't so many as those whose alignment and discipline don't match," Ingram points out, "but they're common enough, and clairvoyance is an alignment, not a discipline. Lightning-aligned metallurgist would be the easiest to find, I imagine."

"I agree. Unfortunately there are no records of such a death within the church." For all that necromancers are not well understood among the greater mage community, they are one of the few solid institutions: births are not generally registered, but deaths are noted, if only because most mages do not die naturally. One must always track dangers. And, of course, many mages do not wish to bother with the expense and difficulty of a funeral, and so are quite willing to donate corpses to the church in exchange for a little something.

Ingram frowns. "Then perhaps no one knows about it yet."

Kian nods. "Or the body passed into mortal hands. Metallurgy is not limited to mages; it's possible they passed in non-magical circles. There is an earth-intent mage recorded, but nothing was missing from the corpse, so it's likely there is another yet unfound."

"And no one would be able to tell someone clairvoyant," Ingram murmurs.

"Ironic, isn't it?" Kian says cheerfully. "One needs a clairvoyant to see whether the deceased is one."

"Or you could reanimate them," Ingram points out.

"Whyever would we do that for every John and Jane who passes into our hands?"

"Practice in reanimating?" Ingram suggests, in a tone which seems more thoughtful than leading. "What *do* necromancers do with the corpses that come into their care?"

"The same thing most coroners do," Kian says dryly. "Any one of us could walk into a morgue and perform the same work, Healer Ingram; when one wants answers as to a death, there is truly only one place to go. It's simply that mages are less curious about such answers than non-mages."

"Curious," Ingram murmurs. "Then we're relying on the metallurgist."

"Quite," says Kian dryly, "Metallurgists aren't thick upon the ground in London. The first place to investigate may be the Historical Metallurgy Society."

"That does sound like somewhere a mage might wish to inhabit," Ingram agrees. "Is there a website?"

"There is. That's how I found it in the first place." Kian makes to rise, sees her eyebrow lift, and instead opts to point toward the table near the head of the cot. "I have a tablet." Ingram goes to retrieve it herself, while Kian continues. "In the interim, I made a friend in the coroner who autopsied Gregory, and have a dinner appointment with her for tomorrow night. It may be that she has acquaintances in other morgues who will be able to tell us whom they've found on their tables." Her eyebrow is still lifted when she returns to the table, and Kian chooses to ignore it in favour of unlocking the tablet. "If you would be so good as to begin that search, I would appreciate it. I have some other appointments to set up. Before then, however ..."

He'd begun some other leads before he went to sleep, and when he unlocks the tablet the first thing on it is a page for Carruthers Business Advisory at Companies Houses.

"Did you find much about the business?" Ingram asks.

"No, not much at all. I know a technomancer in Ireland. She agreed to trace the money."

"That's illegal," Ingram points out in the tone of someone acutely aware of their own words.

Kian laughs. "Our existence is illegal, Healer Ingram."

Verna hasn't replied yet, but if Kian recalls she is lightning-aligned, though not a metallurgist; so he shoots her a quick follow-up question and then closes his email and hands the tablet over, and Ingram takes it while eyeing him curiously. "What are you going to do?"

"There are a number of collectors in London," Kian explains, checking his pocketwatch. It isn't *too* late, yet. "Some of them deal specifically in antique weapons. If we can't find the owner of this blade, perhaps we can find where he received it. Failing that, it may be worth trying to sneak into the scene on Tower Hill Road to find a piece of the car that tried to run me down. There's likely a witch somewhere in London willing to perform a scry, if we can't do so ourselves."

"Or," says Ingram, "we can call the police to ask whether they've found any trace of the car."

"Or that," Kian agrees. "Shall we?"

The next steps involve significantly more busy-work than Kian ordinarily enjoys, particularly in subpar circumstances; but he's anticipating the satisfaction when the situation is resolved. Particularly when he knows who would burn down a healer's clinic. He doesn't like being on the radar of someone who doesn't adhere to social conventions. They're wildcards, and this one has proven themselves dangerous.

Fortunately, there are a number of antiquity collectors in London, and enough of them haven't yet retired, and are interested in seeing what he has. Unfortunately, this means walking — or at least leaving the hotel. Ingram is none too pleased about this, but they dine late before they go, to sate both healing needs and Ingram's sense of responsibility; and after both meal and sleep she's able to feed judicious energy into the injuries. It still feels oddly cold and cutting, like sunlight on ice; and Kian firmly sets aside the memory of her leaning against his chest that morning, head down and hand warm.

On this occasion Ingram insists on their going together; and the main issue with this is the fact that the skeleton gets up to follow them as they make for the door. Ingram's lack of clothes is less so. Kian had sent her clothes to be laundered after she fell asleep; and they were, from the time she rose, waiting for attention on one of the armchairs. Kian only submits to alerting Ingram they are there when she declares her intent to come with him and then frowns as she realises she can't very well do so in a bathrobe. Her focus on research and lack of attention to anything else had only been amusing up until that point: silence beyond that would have been cruel.

So: the skeleton. Kian stops with his hand on the knob and turns, as does Ingram, and they both look at the skeleton, and then at each other.

"Would it stay if you told it?" Ingram asks, and Kian restrains a grimace to a downward pull of his mouth.

"I'd like to say I could be certain," he admits, "but to be frank, I'm not sure." There's something — odd about the skeleton. Something beyond the faint glow in its skull and the attention it gives, something beyond the rude gestures it had given him, gingerly like they were something unfamiliar and only recently learned. Though that is terrifying enough; reanimations lacking brains are not capable of learning, and even those still in possession of such faculties aren't guaranteed.

No. There's a sense, when Kian is close to it, like a quietly humming chord somewhere just behind him. It could conceivably be the bond — but it shouldn't be audible in such a way. Not like this; not without something to resonate *back*. A soul-reaver, by nature, cleaves soul from body irrevocably.

Ingram turns to the skeleton.

"Stay," she says firmly, somewhere between addressing a dog and addressing a child. The skeleton looks at her, and when Kian turns the knob, it takes another step. Kian sighs.

"I suppose we could do with having the third with us, just in case." The other two knives are those he's rewrapped to take to one of the experts, spinning an almost-falsehood about finding them in a drawer in a dead associate's desk. It's a lie only in that the office had not been Gregory's. Kian is hoping to get more information about the glass blade out of this.

"Just in case of what?"

"Just in case we need to use it, probably. Please present." Kian turns, reaching for his phone, and the skeleton gives him a measuring look before lifting the blade, how nice. "So that I am *not* taking a picture of your ribs." The skeleton gives him another Look and holds the knife out over the coffee-table, as if it's laying down, and while that makes for a good picture it means the skeleton still hasn't released it. Not that Kian would have tried to snatch it up if the skeleton had; that seems unwise at this juncture.

"In that case, you're going to need to lend it a suit," Ingram says, and Kian truly cannot help the way his face sours.

"Why don't we just give it dear Gregory's clothes, hm?" He is not wasting a suit on a skeleton who can't bear to put down a lethal weapon.

"*My* clothes," Ingram corrects, but she goes to the bag in which the church had returned those clothes, returned also by the hotel after laundering, and pulls out the clothes Gregory had worn, right down to the wellies. The skeleton looks at her and makes no move to pick up what she lays down; and so after a moment Ingram sighs and shakes out the sweatpants. "One foot after another, come on."

Kian opts not to get involved, judging three to be too many cooks while a bare blade is around; and though the skeleton is awkward about it, it at least does not have to worry about balance while Ingram helps it pull pants on, followed by hoodie, wellies and scarf. It still looks absurdly skinny, and the hoodie only barely pulls down far enough to hide the way the trackpants hang off hips. Still alien — but honestly, who on Earth would be able to tell? It's dark now, and no one is going to look at someone skinny in a hoodie and think they're a skeleton. At least not once the soul-reaver is carefully and safely stowed in the front pocket.

"There, now we shan't be in danger at all," Kian says brightly, and turns toward the door. "Shall we?"

Fourteen

WINDOW SHOPPING

Kian's brightness has not at all reassured Rosemary. One thing to be walking the streets with a skeleton animated mostly by the organs in it, the remnants of a cocky young man who ought to have had more time to grow out of his belligerent hedonism; another entirely to be shadowed by something strange enough it gives even the local expert on the topic some pause. She swears she can feel the skeleton observing her as it follows them, trailing like some *exceptionally* peculiar guard-dog.

It may be her imagination. Certainly there are no processes of life for her to detect.

As a small mercy, the soul-reaving blade stays tucked in the pocket of the hoodie.

Rosemary looks to Kian for direction, once they're out on the street. He's the one who's been calling antiquities dealers, and therefore, in theory, the one with a plan regarding where to go.

After a moment to assess he picks a direction and sets out, and Rosemary falls into step a pace behind him, watching his gait carefully. She'd put in the extra effort on the healing, and she knows from intimate awareness of the inner workings of his leg that it's near to completely functioning as it should, but she's still vaguely suspicious that Kian will strain something.

He makes use of the cane. She appreciates that.

When she's satisfied with that she lengthens her stride to keep about even with him, and Kian glances over with a raised eyebrow as if to imply he knows exactly what she was doing. "I trust you're satisfied with your work, Healer Ingram?"

She is. Rosemary nods, a quick sharp jerk of a motion. "Do say something if you notice any further pain," she says, and with any luck her tone is severe enough that he will take her seriously.

"Of course," Kian murmurs. Rosemary mostly believes him.

The first antiquity shop they visit has two sections: one in the front, full of rust and chintz in equal measures, and one in the back, with quiet glass cases protecting more carefully preserved items. Here an older man with a well-restored pince-nez hems over the two knives Kian shows him, venturing that he hasn't seen anything like the glass-and-metal blade, but that the plainer of the two might be Egyptian in origin — the blade Rosemary had originally taken for some old, dark and pitted metal is actually stone.

Kian has a troubled look on his face after that.

"Flint-knapping went out of style almost as soon as metalwork started spreading widely, wherever there were resources. This isn't

126

anything special, magically speaking," he explains, rather plainly. Rosemary has to assume he noted the stone blade when he was studying them, and is now elucidating for her benefit. "I *hope* it is from a period when someone simply didn't have the coin for a metal blade, or we are looking at something several millennia old."

Rosemary considers this, lines up some pieces in her head from what Kian hasn't said. "Either very old, or belonging to someone with reason to emulate very old styles, then. Can you think of anything that would require a stone blade specifically?"

There's some quiet as they walk and as Kian thinks this over. Rosemary grows accustomed to this more even rhythm of footsteps and cane, and the determined dragging scuffle of skeleton behind. She tries not to think about it; and then she recognises that she cannot afford to not think about it, and renews her attention.

"Nothing immediately comes to mind," Kian says finally. "I would say something for lack of conductivity, but the hilt has metal ornaments. Somehow I doubt our man is lightning-aligned, with this assortment of knives."

It isn't an auspicious start.

The next stop they make is a little astray from only antiquities — a young man with dark skin and a riotously-coloured assortment of braids has kept his family's glass shop open a little later for them, out of sheer curiosity. Kian only shows him the glass knife, for perhaps obvious reasons, and the young man is clearly delighted. Some bright lights and careful observation have him pointing out the faintest of impurities and flaws. "Normally," he adds, "you wouldn't get an edge this fine on glass except by breaking it, but this edge is angled the wrong way for a break. It might have been filed down, but don't quote me on that. I'd like to meet whoever made it, though."

Rosemary compresses her mouth. That certainly wouldn't be a good idea.

"Any idea on the age?" Kian wonders, leaning in.

The young man shakes his head. "Can't rule anything out. It's probably younger than a hundred years, given the quality. No maker's mark, little wear, no fractures. Whoever had this before was taking care of it. You're not looking to sell, are you?" This a little wistfully. "It's probably one of a kind."

"My apologies," Kian says. Rosemary doesn't think he sounds very sorry. "If I ever *am* looking to part with it, I shall look you up."

"Thanks anyhow. Cheers, mate."

Out again into the night, and Kian's frown is deeper this time, though he smooths it away as soon as he catches Rosemary looking. "This hasn't been a terribly productive evening so far, I'm afraid," he says lightly. "Third time's the charm?"

Rosemary doubts this, too, and she can't *quite* control the way she grimaces, but she perseveres.

The third time is not the charm. Their third visit is to a woman in a vastly upscale shop, ageless in that particular way of the immortal disciplines, with faint crow's feet about her eyes that might have been there for a year or thirty years. She doesn't have anything helpful to say about the first two knives, and coos wistfully over the picture of the third, evidently disappointed.

"This one's *beautiful*," she says, looking more at Rosemary than at Kian. "Look at that weathering, it's aged and coloured a bit but I can tell from here that hasn't damaged it. Oh, but are you sure it belongs with the other two?"

"They're from the same set," Kian says, "but their provenance could well be different."

The woman tuts, shakes her head. "If I had it in my hands I could tell you more. Right off, I can only tell you that it isn't metal, it's bone. It's very cleverly made to look like metal, but if you look it's got a bit of a grain—and see, the way it's sheared just here isn't damage, it's how it was shaped in the first place—" She indicates a spot along the curve Rosemary had honestly overlooked. "I couldn't even begin to guess what bone it is without touching it, nothing I know off the top of my head would age this shade. I'd be happy to see you come back if you can — where did you say it was?"

"There was a mild ownership dispute," Rosemary says blandly, since the woman is addressing her before Kian still. "It's in someone else's hands right now, but we may be able to resolve that."

The skeleton shuffles drearily in the corner. Rosemary is more than happy to withdraw, with that reminder looming over her shoulder.

Rosemary doesn't catch Kian frowning this time, but she doubts he's any more pleased with their progress than she is.

Their fourth destination is less prepossessing than the others; they aren't visiting a shopfront, but someone's home, it looks like, an apartment in a tower of other apartments. "Glad you could go out of your way," the woman who answers the door says, stepping aside to let them in without explicitly tendering invitation. She's very short, but has an aggressive sort of cheer about her. "I know this can't have been convenient, but I couldn't pass up getting a look. Have a seat?"

Her home has the sort of simple style which is deeply expensive for the quality involved. Rosemary knows the type; it has her feeling out of place all over again. Delicately she takes up a seat on the offered couch. The skeleton loiters just behind her, hood hopefully far enough down to avoid any awkward questions — Rosemary doesn't dare look up and back, lest she draw attention to it.

She doesn't like it behind her like this, either. The back of her neck prickles almost continuously.

Kian opts for an armchair a little closer to the low wooden coffee-table, leans forward to roll out the knives. They're in good company: much of the decor of the room is antique swords, displayed everywhere with pride. "We haven't had much luck establishing provenance," he says. "Anything at all you can say would be helpful."

"Kian, right?" the woman asks, testing pronunciation. At his nod, she offers a hand to shake. "My father-in-law always had good things to say about you."

If Rosemary's any judge, the expression on his face is polite disbelief.

"Good," she clarifies, "not necessarily nice."

"Ah," Kian says. "Yes, that would follow. Ms. O'Briain, my associate, Healer Ingram —"

An exchange of nods. Rosemary leans over for a quick handshake.

"— and our security-minded companion." Kian gestures behind Rosemary, evidently having decided that not 'introducing' the skeleton would be too peculiar. "He doesn't say much."

"Call me Maddie," she says, and looks askance at the skeleton before settling back on the knives. "Well. Let me go over these a bit, and I'll see what I can tell you."

She has a deft touch, Rosemary notes, and her brown fingers are graceful and sure. There's never any fear that she'll cut herself, even as she runs an inquisitive fingertip along the rippled edge of the stone knife. Rosemary waits with her hands folded and still, terribly aware of the passage of time. It was already dark by the time they got out, and walking has not been all that efficient except that it saves them the issue of parking. Time marches on; and yet, with the skeleton behind her, the passage fairly crawls. Every further moment is another moment something may go wrong, beginning with the peculiar animation and ending somewhere beyond any possible future murder attempts.

Maddie starts talking again with the stone knife still in her hands. "This is interesting," she says, "because it's definitely a few different eras. The blade is very, very old — I definitely couldn't tell you how old — but the hilt, the metal and all these engravings here, those are much newer. Within the last few hundred years. So some of the original style has changed."

"I missed that," Kian murmurs, sounding as piqued as he ever does. "Can you tell anything further despite that?"

As she sets the knife down again, Maddie shrugs lazily. "Maybe. Depending what the original hilt looked like, this could have come from a few different places, but based on the relative broadness and this curve, here, I would *guess* Egypt. You'd want to look into the stone to be sure."

'Maybe Egypt' is one thing; hearing it from two sources who haven't spoken to each other is another, slightly more promising thing. Kian either doesn't agree or knows something Rosemary doesn't. "What about this one?" he asks, indicating the glass knife, his brow still faintly knit.

"Weird," Maddie pronounces before she's even touched it. She picks it up and turns it over, sights along the back of the blade and whistles low and impressed. "This is ridiculous. It's either rarely used or very well taken care of, and that's all I've got. No one actually *uses* glass knives, you know? There was a time when you'd use glass for scalpels, and you get some obsidian ones still today, but mostly at this point metalworking technology is good enough. This is the stupidest beautiful thing I've ever seen."

Rosemary can't quite help smiling over the way she puts that. Maddie sets it down again, and her gaze is all over thoughtful now, distant in the direction of the glass knife. "Looking at the rest of it — copper is a good conductor, so's silver. Glass isn't, but it's interesting how the metal runs almost the full length of the blade in ornament."

There's something about the pattern of metal over glass that's catching Rosemary's eye, now that she's been drawn to study it more closely. Almost blood vessels, not quite. She holds her tongue over it, not quite sure what it means yet, or if she's only imagining it for the brain's tendency to fill in familiar patterns. Still: it's something.

"If you look at the metaphysical properties you might turn more up," Maddie says. "Off the top of my head I know copper is associated with healing a lot, but that's about it. Oh — and neither of these is a fighting knife, they're both balanced terribly. They're art or ceremonial pieces, absolutely."

"Hm," Kian says. "All of that is helpful, I think. I appreciate you taking the time."

"Pleasure's mine," Maddie says. "Give me a bit of your time somewhere down the line and we'll call it square. Oh — actually, Healer Ingram, which side do you practice on?"

"A little of both," Rosemary says automatically. "I'm fully licensed according to modern medical standards, but the larger portion of my clientele is magical." She pats her pockets looking for a card out of habit, and her face freezes as she recalls. She'll certainly not be able to resume operations at the same address for some time. "My practice may be — moving, in any case. I can recommend someone, potentially?"

"I see." Maddie does not sound as if she sees. "Well, it's not urgent; if you don't mind giving me your number, we can talk about it later."

Business is business. Rosemary confers with Maddie on this for a few minutes, arranging to talk details later, and they exchange contact information — Rosemary discovers that her full name is Madrigal, which explains the nickname — and by the time they're done Kian has rolled up the knives and the skeleton is shifting after him. "If it's not something I can handle, I'm sure I can refer you," Rosemary says. "For now, though, I think we may be in a rush?"

"Sure, no trouble." Maddie sees them out. There's the click of the lock behind them, which Rosemary personally thinks is wise. Back to the street it is.

"Do you have other stops in mind?" Rosemary asks, on their way down and out.

Kian shakes his head. "There were a few more potentials, but they were longer shots, based on their area of expertise. We have a start, at least."

It isn't much of one, but at least they know what they don't know, and that is in some ways just as valuable. "Two different people have now recommended Egypt," Rosemary says as they exit the building. "I suppose the mismatch tells us that our problem is well-travelled?"

"Among other things." Kian takes a breath of the night air, and visibly draws himself up to a cheerier face. "This keeps getting more interesting."

Interesting is in this case not a compliment, Rosemary thinks, and matches Kian as they go, the skeleton never more than a pace or two behind.

FIFTEEN

JACKALS IN THE DARK

They leave Madrigal's with the moon now far overhead and much of the traffic having subsided, to the degree London's traffic ever subsides. Kian remains quiet and thoughtful, and Ingram remains likewise quiet; Kian can only assume thoughtful. He had honestly thought they would get more about the glass knife than the other; the fact that the glass is such a confusing non-entity does not speak well for the extent of their investigation.

Twice now Egypt has been mentioned. That and the conductivity of the glass knife is causing an uneasy thought to lurk in Kian's mind; the sort where conclusion is just out of reach, for lack of expertise or imagination. It is not a pleasant feeling.

"Well," says Ingram eventually, after they're a number of blocks away, "where now?"

"Back to the Chamberlain, I should think," says Kian soberly. Cheer is slightly difficult to muster at this juncture.

"We don't know anything, do we?" Her tone is, once more, business-like as opposed to any of her other options; in this case, Kian might have expected 'dispirited'.

"On the contrary, we know quite a bit," Kian disagrees. "It's simply that none of that knowledge connects to each other — yet."

"Do you think the knife being Egyptian is important?" Kian is about to answer this when there's a whisper of a tune, like a reed instrument; thready and drawn, and unnervingly piercing. He pauses, head not turning as he casts his gaze along the street, and Ingram moves a few paces more before stopping herself. "What is it?"

His heart's pounding. That is — not good. Indeterminate dread is *not good*. Kian steps closer to Ingram, keeping his breathing even with some effort; and the skeleton rattles closer still, head turned toward the shadow of a lane they'd been about to pass. That, also, is not good.

"I don't believe we're alone, Healer Ingram," Kian says softly, and the words feel rather as though they're coming from numbed lips.

Ingram studies him for a moment, and then sounds surprised as she says: "Are you afraid?"

"I choose to be flattered by the implication that such a thing is so difficult to believe." The reed instrument continues to play, so light and long on the notes that it seems cutting — the sort of cutting to make his breath catch, for all that it's supposed to be a sound. Ingram doesn't seem to hear it, so it's not *merely* a sound. "I suspect we may wish to choose another route."

He steps away from the lane, but before he can turn to find a different way down the street there's another low thread of tune, counter-playing equally long and slow as the first. Kian's heart thuds doubly-loud, and when he exhales slowly, vying for calm, it shakes. There's more than one.

"What are they?" Ingram asks, very softly and with a faint tremor; and that tells him that she is also now being affected, if not able to hear. "Ghosts?"

"No ghost can broadcast like this," Kian answers, reaching back, and is gratified but not surprised when he feels her hand slide into his. If they're cut off, then the best way is forward — though safety may not be had at the hotel. No; they're best heading somewhere they may be able to fight reanimation with reanimation. He moves across the street, heading for the distant dim-glow that is the Hill and the Tower. Ingram grips his hand and follows close, and the skeleton clatters along after.

"What can?"

"There are a number — but after our recent conversations I would hazard it's something Egyptian."

She absorbs that without a word, and Kian doesn't look back to see what expression she might be wearing. "What kinds of things from Egypt can do this?"

It's an effort to keep his pace even, but Kian perseveres, not daring to look around into the hanging shadows of the evening. They pass a lane and just the passing makes him break out in cold sweat, and it takes all his willpower not to break into a run then and there; and Ingram presses up against his side before checking herself.

"I'm not sure."

Shadows or something else? Something worse? Kian's no Egyptologist — he hasn't even spent time in their temples. Some say necromancy as they know it has its roots in Egypt; but humankind has ever been fascinated with death. Still, it's hard to deny that Egypt has a deeper fabric than most places. None of this helps them now.

Can Carruthers be a necromancer? As far back as their records go, he could have left one of the temples centuries before and they wouldn't even know to track him. Just his having an English name means little. This also doesn't help them now.

They move further along the street, and Kian's back itches with the feeling of looming danger. The soft, haunting tune is carried by four instruments now — four that he can pick out, reverberating against his soul. It's ... odd that he should be able to hear them this way. The tunes that resonate in the soul are specific to individuals; these form melodies. It's as though they're missing parts of themselves and instead vie to fill in for each other.

Kian has not habitually tried to summon souls which aren't in one piece — at least not on purpose.

Something steps out from a lane ahead, and it seems at first two-dimensional; as if it has to peel itself away from the opening, long tendrils of limbs stretching before snapping back into place. Ingram draws in a sharp breath and pulls back, and Kian doesn't: he grips her hand tighter and strides straight through the silhouette, and it feels like plunging through sunlight and the scent of reeds on water, and sand as far as the eye can see —

Street, and smog, and darkness, and Kian continues to hurry them along. That's not what was pursuing them. At least, that's not *all* of what was pursuing them.

"What —?"

"Do not stop," Kian tells her tersely. If these are Egyptian — ghosts — for lack of the correct term — then there are strict rules governing their existence. Egyptian funerals are among the strictest. It's unlikely these have just randomly chosen to pursue them, so someone is controlling them. Ordinarily he might try blood to abscond with the reanimation, but he doesn't dare stop long enough to get that close to one of them; and may not even be able to. At least at the Tower he would be in a place of power with other potential reanimations about —

Something dark and low streaks past them on the other side of the street, and Kian can't help but jerk toward it; and when he turns there's something else again before them, far more solid than the shadow, made of flashing teeth and claws and jackal's head but human body. Kian jumps back and Ingram stumbles against the wall beside them, and while snatching for the head of his cane Kian drops the leather roll in which the knives are stowed. The figure shifts from two-legged to four, smoothly ducking under the slash of his narrow-edged blade, and in a moment has the roll in jaws and darts off past them down the street.

Kian whirls to follow despite his own warning to Ingram, and behind them the street seems dim, and there's silhouettes upright on the pavement, with heads misshapen from what they ought to be. There's more than four. He can no longer pick out how many instruments are there in the tune.

"What are they?" Ingram asks again, shaken and still gripping the wall, and gaze fixed on the silhouettes. Kian can't think to answer. There *is* a name for them, he knows — he just can't think of it. Unreasoning fright has made his head agonisingly blank. "They're coming for us," Ingram adds in a tone too detached to be anything but terrified herself.

There's something missing in all this, something —

Where is the skeleton?

The skeleton. With the soul-reaver. Kian would curse himself if he felt inclined for a lasting punishment. They'd cut him off from the *soul-reaver*, and all the while he'd been wondering how he was meant to drive them off.

Irritable spite is not quite the salve for panic but it's enough to cut through, and though Kian does not particularly want to get *closer* to those things, he nevertheless steps in front of Ingram.

"What are you —"

"Stay behind me," he tells her without turning, and his voice is tight rather than terrified, which is something of an improvement. He hums a chord and then starts singing, the same that he'd sung when he pricked the skeleton's spine with the knife; this time not murmured or half-hummed, but low and deep. It clashes with the long note of the tune he's hearing, but neither falters; and for a few steps there's songs vying for space in the street while the reanimations walk ever closer. One of the streetlights nearest illuminates those in front, light shining off dark fur and a jackal's face, and an ear flickering as if there's an annoying sound which won't go away.

It's carrying a flail, he notices with detach when it's barely more than three paces away, which is just lovely; and then out of the nearest lane comes a furious clatter of bone and a streak of yellow wellies and dirty-white scrubs, and the skeleton barrels straight into the crowd, reaver held high. Immediately there's an unearthly jackal's shriek and those nearest scatter, except for one unfortunate which is struck by the blade. That one's scream makes Kian's whole body goosebump, and as if there's seams the reaver had cut its body splits, its parts departing in a rush of feathers and shadow.

The rest of them circle, snarling and calling at one another; and then, finally, backing away when the skeleton makes as if to lunge again. It turns toward them with naked blade still in hand and skull sockets infused green, and in the moment looks almost put out.

Kian exhales, does not manage to resist the shiver, and says, "There you are. I noticed they'd lost you. Don't put that away; just make sure no one can see it at a glance."

His tone is rather less cheerful than he could wish, but given that his heart is still racing like he's just woken from a nightmare, he'll forgive himself. Kian turns to Ingram, still pressed against the wall; and she takes a breath and seems to realise that she *is*, in fact, pressed against the wall, and pushes herself off it, shaking her head and brushing off her clothes with shaking hands.

"They're afraid of the skeleton," she says, and then corrects herself before Kian can: "No. They're afraid of the reaver, aren't they?"

Kian nods. "Egyptian death has a great deal to do with a soul's constituent parts — more than any other. Reavers are the only things which can cut a soul; ergo, it's one of the few things which can hurt them."

"I thought death is death," Ingram murmurs, and it's not *precisely* a question; but it's the sort of question wherein someone is asking without asking.

"Culture is interpretation, Healer Ingram," Kian answers, "and cultures all view death differently. Come." He holds out his hand and after a moment she takes it, and it's difficult to tell whom is gripping whom more tightly. Kian opts to say nothing on that as they turn to move back up the street.

"They're going to come after us again, aren't they?" Ingram says after a moment. "If they were merely after the knives, they would have given up just as soon as they had them."

"Most likely," Kian admits. "I can set up a few wards, but I think our best defence is keeping our friend here close — and to call the temple in Cairo as soon as we're indoors. We've irked Carruthers, it seems."

Ingram nods and asks no further questions, and they return in shaky silence to the Chamberlain.

Sixteen

NOWHERE NEAR THE NILE

I t occurs to Rosemary about halfway back to the Chamberlain that she might like to let go of Kian's hand. Potentially. Eventually.

The creatures, the not-ghosts that had attacked them, had brought an unnatural fear with them, threading past her hard-maintained composure and driving her to seek reassurance. Sternly Rosemary reminds herself that Kian reached out first, and it is within her purview to provide some limited comfort to patients. Maintaining a good bedside manner is important.

This is a little more than that. Besides, she would be lying to herself if she tried to claim that she had not benefited from that hold. It's only that now she doesn't know how to politely let go. Surely any way she tries to untwine their fingers will result in Kian noticing exactly what she's doing. And if he hasn't let go yet ...

It occurs to Rosemary that she is being consumed with nonsense. Likely some leftover emotion from the attack. A hand is only a hand.

In their room again, Kian solves the dilemma for her by needing his hand for the room key. From there he goes irritably in search of contact information, leaving Rosemary to handle the skeleton.

The skeleton does not seem very inclined to give up the knife. Well, they've been coping with that problem already. Rosemary considers the problem of clothes or lack thereof — is there truly any reason it should ever be without them? Save, of course, that they are her spares, and now among the very few things she yet owns. She studies it for a little while, watches it pick a spot in the room from which it can 'see' both her and Kian.

She doesn't really wish to argue with it about the wellies. Or at all.

So there's nothing to do really but watch the skeleton. Rosemary settles at the table they'd had the files spread across and observes it. Distantly she observes, too, that her hands are a little shaky now that the adrenaline has passed, that now she has come near to death and the possibility of leaving Rowan alone in the world twice over in as many days. It would be beneficial to set aside some time to process all of this. Possibly to speak to a professional — she doesn't immediately know anyone on the magical side of things, but she's sure she could secure a recommendation from a colleague.

Kian has returned before she can think too much further on that. Gently, Rosemary puts the thoughts away. She learned about being fine when needs must nearly half her life ago, and it's served her decently well. She can work through all this later. There will be a later.

"I presume you would prefer this be conducted via speakerphone," Kian says. He has a number dialled; now he starts the call, toggles it to speaker, and sets the phone on the table between them.

Rosemary nods an agreement. "If I'm going to be helpful, there's no sense in secondhand information, not when I'm right here," she says. "The more data, the better. I suppose if there's something that's very private —"

"We have rather crossed that bridge, Healer Ingram," Kian says.

She means to inquire precisely what he means by that, but then the ringing stops as someone picks up the phone. It sounds like a person yawning, and then there's a light female voice, a greeting in a language which sounds vaguely familiar but which Rosemary can't quite understand.

"Good morning," Kian says, and waits a moment. Rosemary wonders if the language is for her benefit or not.

"Ah, Cairo Temple," comes from the other end, lightly accented. "Abdel speaking, and you've used the necromancers-only international line so I'm going to give you the benefit of the doubt and assume you don't know what time it is here."

"Cleric Kian Ó Maolomhnaigh," Kian says, and Rosemary thinks she may have nailed the particular twist of vowels that marks the Irish pronunciation distinct from the anglicisation. "Calling from London. I'm aware it's late, but this is urgent."

"This had better be good," Abdel says, but she sounds more alert now, inasmuch as the tinny phone connection allows for such nuance. "Urgent how, Cleric?"

"My partner and I were attacked." Kian has upped his estimation of Rosemary while she wasn't looking, apparently. "The attackers were mostly shadow; when they took solid form, they were misshapen humans, some with the heads of beasts, specifically jackals. One carried a flail in what looked like an old Egyptian style. And when they weren't solid, they seemed to separate into pieces." There's a thoughtfulness as he speaks, evidently being careful about picking the best words for the job. "Discrete fragments not whole on their own, I think."

"... You're sure?" Abdel's voice has dropped about an octave into something terse and concerned. "Was there anything else?"

"Sure enough. We could hear their songs," Kian says. He rests his chin in his hand, and his gaze is distant with recollection. Rosemary appreciates his equanimity, so soon after such an attack. "They didn't sound right. Incomplete, shall we say. Fragments of a larger melody."

"Please hold," Abdel says. The phone click-thumps, and there's silence.

"As much as I was hoping for urgency," Kian murmurs, "*that* sort of response does not inspire a great deal of reassurance."

Rosemary has to agree. "You did take pictures of all of the knives, didn't you?"

Kian nods, gestures to his phone. "We are not wholly without recourse, although, of course, I would prefer we had managed to keep them. And of course we still have the reaver, and our ... friend."

"Perhaps they will be able to shed some light on that anomaly as well." Rosemary sits back, drawing one leg up to her chest. She aches everywhere and is only now starting to notice it. Absently she slips a thread of focus and power through her own muscles, easing the worst of the strain so she'll still be mostly functional in the near future.

"Perhaps," Kian echoes, though he doesn't sound exceptionally hopeful on the topic.

It's another several minutes before the phone is picked up again. Rosemary would hate to think of the bill Kian must be accumulating on this call, except that he's made it fairly clear he can write most of this off as a justifiable workplace expense. His fingers tap now and then, to some unheard beat.

"Here, here — ah. Hello?" The person answering sounds male, but that's about all Rosemary can tell; she wouldn't care to estimate age on this alone. "Kian, was it?"

"And my associate, Healer Ingram," Kian provides. "You're on speakerphone."

"That's fine, that's fine. You can call me Geddo." Rosemary is having trouble nailing down an impression, beyond the general assumption that he must be some sort of expert. She stays quiet for the time being; Kian has introduced her, so there's really no need to chime in. "Now. Go over the details of this attack again, please?"

Kian does. He catches details of the attack Rosemary had missed — it makes sense now, why he had reacted before she did, if she couldn't hear an accompanying music that he could. She remembers mostly that they were creatures like shadows, like jackals, like half-made people that moved at the wrong rhythm, driven by things other than muscles and blood. Geddo makes quiet go-on sorts of sounds while Kian is speaking, and otherwise refrains from interrupting until Kian has completed the account.

He hasn't mentioned the knives yet. Rosemary assumes that's coming, since the knife was one of their best initial reasons for assuming some Egyptian tradition was involved.

"Have you anything which Kian hasn't already, Healer Ingram?"

It takes her an embarrassingly long few moments to recognise that Geddo has addressed her, caught up as she is in thought processes. "The one we walked through was warm, but carried scents and impressions," Rosemary says, reviewing. "In my limited experience thus far, Kian's use of shadows has been warm, but completely devoid of other sensory feedback. Further, I noticed afterward a lingering chill, atypical for the current weather. I believe Kian has been otherwise comprehensive thus far."

"I see." Geddo sighs, and there's a sober note to his voice. "It sounds from all your descriptions like these were akh, which they should not be."

"Akh?" Rosemary repeats in an undertone, with a quick glance to Kian to establish if this would be necromantic in general or specifically Egyptian. Kian shakes his head, a tiny frown only faintly visible but not being smoothed away.

"Suffice to say for now that the akh is a piece of the soul, which arises after a person dies and the proper rites are followed,"

Geddo elaborates. "The ba and the ka come together, and thus is the akh born. They are not the whole of a person, and indeed should not be doing such things in the first place. Think of them, perhaps, as fragmentary ghosts, perverted from their natural selves by whomever holds their bodies and their names. This is ... very wrong. If indeed that is what they are," he tacks on the end, and it seems like it is as much a hope as it is a doubt of their observational capacities.

"They reacted very poorly to a soul-reaver," Kian says, rubbing at the bridge of his nose. He looks tired, in a way he didn't even when he was earlier bleeding out on Rosemary's (forever-gone) clinic floor. "If they are *not* your akh, then they are some ghost of equal properties, fragments of soul and little else."

Rosemary hears Geddo's breath go out in a low hiss. "A soul-reaver. Where did you come by such a thing?"

"Larceny," Kian says, with some dry low twist of sarcasm. "To start from the beginning — we followed the body of a local young cleric who had been murdered. When we found him, the soul-reaver along with two other knives was stored nearby. We took those for study, in addition to returning his body to the church."

"Do you still have it?" Geddo wants to know.

"The reaver, yes. The other two were taken during the attack, though I still have pictures. One of them is glass set in copper and silver, the other stone with wood and metal hilt — multiple sources thought that blade might be old Egyptian in origin, though the hilt is newer." Kian provides the facts in bland sequence, watching the phone as though not certain what to expect from it yet.

"And you know soul-reavers would be bound with blood."
Geddo seems to be getting at something, Rosemary thinks, though she's not sure what.

Kian shakes his head. "Yes, but I've already handled the matter. I overrode the bond as soon as I had the chance to ascertain what it was."

"Hm," Geddo says. "And what about the other two?"

"They didn't carry the same power," Kian says, "and I did not have a great deal of blood available that was not otherwise engaged." He pauses there, and Geddo doesn't say anything, in the particular way some teachers have of *pointedly* not saying anything. Rosemary watches with interest as Kian processes, finally grimaces. "Of course," he says, resigned, a touch bitterly. "Glass and metal. Reflections?"

"So I would suspect," Geddo agrees. "I'd like to see those pictures."

"Certainly. Where can I send them?"

Geddo provides an email address; repeats it, clarifying the spelling helpfully, when Kian asks. Kian meanwhile picks up the phone to work around the call, and within a minute or two the pictures of the knives are on their way to Cairo, and Geddo is making thoughtful noises about them.

Rosemary suspects he is frowning.

"The blade-shape is indeed evocative of old ritual knives," he says finally. "As for the glass, it is a perfect medium for transmission, especially once blood is involved. Transmission of what, I could not say, save that it would surely be immaterial. Magic, or —"

Another pause. "Well. A soul-reaving blade may cut the soul, whether its attachments or its fabric. Yes? That alone would be bad enough, savaging the soul's natural state. But say, then, that a piece of the soul is controlled. This, too, could be moved through blood and glass. And atop all this, such knives would not need necromancy to wield. There is power in the rites, and power in blades held for this long, and power in the bodies and names ..."

Geddo is beginning to paint an alarming picture. Rosemary turns those pieces over thoughtfully, finally speaks up into the leftover silence. "If these akh are pieces of the soul, then they must have come from people originally, correct? Would there be any way to identify them? I don't know that there was anything individually identifiable on them — not that we had the knowledge to recognise, anyway — but if there are specific rites, specific supplies, that would be needed to, ah, manifest the akh in such a way, then perhaps we could track those?"

"I already have an acolyte checking on our burials," Geddo says. "All of our necromancers, too, are fully accounted for. It is more than likely someone very old, with knowledge of the rituals but not one of us. That, however, means that these souls may be of a similar age, not recently dead — you would be looking for canopic jars."

This, at least, is a reference Rosemary can place, even if it's from bad archaeology adventure films. Kian cuts in here. "And those are rather easier to conceal than an entire body." His tone is somewhere between annoyed and grim. "To sum up, we are looking for a potentially very old mage, of indeterminate discipline and alignment, who stayed and studied in Egypt for some unknown early period in his presumably long lifespan. That certainly narrows it down."

"He would need a place to keep the remains," Geddo puts in. "Somewhere appropriately warded, and where others would not chance on it accidentally."

Kian stares blankly for a moment; then there's a brief, vehement murmuring in a language Rosemary doesn't recognise. "The *freezer*. I didn't think about the rest of the space it must have occupied."

Rosemary follows his train of thought, this time: the morgue-like drawer in Carruthers's office had to go somewhere, and presumably if his office had been directly next to another, the neighbour would have objected to the corpse on the desk. If the space was already cooled, it would be a good place to store any sort of remains, preserved organs included. "If there was anything, it will likely be gone by now," she notes.

"Of course." Kian shakes his head. "Well. I suppose knowing is something." He doesn't sound best pleased with it all the same.

"Knowing is always something better than not," Geddo agrees, though he surely can't have all the context. "Here, then. When we have completed the assessment of our tombs, we will inform you of the result. I suspect your problem is not affiliated with our temple even in that small way, but we would be remiss not to check. As for handling things where you are — if you wish to prevent the akh from being used against you again, you will need to liberate whatever physical remains there are, as well as their names. We can see to their safe passage for you."

"But of course we will need to obtain them first." Kian nods, apparently unsurprised by this. "Naturally. If you think of anything else ...?"

"It benefits us all for you to know if something else comes to mind," Geddo says, which is close enough to a yes that Kian doesn't object. "Yes. We can see about rendering aid, but the London temple ..."

Kian sighs. "They are not best pleased at the moment, I think," he says, "and unlikely to be happier for foreign interference, even if it is between necromancers. Still — forgiveness, rather than permission?"

"Mmh." It's little more than a grunt. Geddo, Rosemary senses, is not convinced. "We shall see. Please don't hesitate to call again if you find further information — though a daylight hour would be better."

"That you will have to take up with the akh," Kian says lightly.

"Perhaps I shall," Geddo says.

He might even be serious.

Farewells are said, and the call ended, leaving Kian staring at the dark phone as though it owes him something, and Rosemary more concerned than when she had started.

Seventeen

Music in the Walls

It's been quite a while since anyone could make Kian feel like a young student lacking breadth of experience, but given to whom he suspects they'd been speaking, perhaps that's to be expected. Mages in the immortal disciplines have not yet discovered an upper end to their lifespans: but few of them reach an age where the literal number of years lived becomes absurd. He knows the temple in Cairo is home to one such mage. It's said no one can remember their high priest's name anymore, he's so old.

Kian does not much like the return of feeling as though he's disappointed a respected teacher. Particularly as it's someone he's never, in truth, met before now.

"Kian."

It's Ingram's voice which makes him look up from the phone, and the ever-so-faintly raised eyebrow which makes him check himself. Clearly, he'd almost fallen to brooding. This is very nearly unconscionable. He summons a smile, faint though it is. "Healer Ingram. Would you care to discover whether the hotel provides room service at this late hour? At the very least, perhaps hot chocolate?"

She absorbs this, and then nods, and then says: "Is this a subtle way of getting me out of the way?"

"Heaven forfend," says Kian. "I was thinking the Harry Potter books aren't all that inaccurate as to the fortifying nature of chocolate. And that if I'm going to ward the room, I'd rather do it after we've been visited by room service."

"Very well," Ingram says, sounding as if she'd really rather not be amused. "I could do with a calming drink."

She rises and Kian does also, almost out of habit; he wants for his tablet, anyway, to check his emails to start with. He'd asked Verna whether she knew any lightning-aligned metallurgists; technomancy doesn't, as a rule, cross much with engineering, but if mages have any sort of consistent community, it usually lays with either alignment or discipline — or sometimes both, as is frequently the case of the church. Sometimes, it just means having two different communities to move between.

Verna has replied, but not answered: names may be forthcoming overnight, as with a destination for the financial trail. It is not much of an update, but it is an update, and judging by the over-use of swearing and emotes, Verna is having the time of her life.

Waiting does not feel like a particularly alluring thought, but Kian spends some time researching Egyptian beliefs and shortly after that hot chocolate arrives from downstairs; and Kian gets to his feet to stretch, very carefully, and consider the dimensions of the room. Blood would not be good for wards, even if he was able to spare some, and given that he's less than twenty-four hours after injury, it's not a risk he particularly wants to take. No; he needs something more substantial. Something which hopefully does not involve too much in the way of defacing private property.

Ingram brings over a mug while he goes to his kit — a flat timber case which opens into a stairway of inks and pens when he lifts the lid. "What are you doing?"

"Wards," Kian answers absently. "These are not merely beings of shadow, though I suspect their shadows — another facet of Egyptian souls — may have been present, if you recall the one through which we walked." Like walking through inverse sunlight: calling to mind everything the shadow is no longer. "So, darkness will not simply do. Light might keep out the shadows, though I doubt it would do much against the akh."

"I don't know much about ward-casting to begin with," Ingram admits. "What are you going to do instead? It had better not —" This, she adds quickly, as if to get in front of his response. "— involve bleeding more."

"I have some sense of survival instinct, thank you," Kian answers with great dignity. "No. There had been music in their presence. Have you ever tried to sing something while something else is playing? That, I think, is where our protection lays."

"Is that what you were doing?" Ingram asks keenly. "When you were singing back at them?"

"Partly. It made them uneasy, if nothing else. The other, greater part was to call our friend to us." He nods in the direction of the skeleton while rifling through his inks. "They made sure to separate us from our defence; but I used that song to create a link to the soul-reaver. It would have been able to hear it, regardless of where we were."

"I see." Ingram sounds thoughtful, as if she truly does see, and motions carefully with one of the mugs. "And those?"

Kian picks out one of the inks and turns with a smile. "The mediums on which music is transcribed matters, Healer Ingram. Though from the looks of Gregory's education, the London Church apparently no longer bothers to offer as extensive an education in metrical linguistics."

"You mentioned that before. What is it?"

"I suppose one could call it a language — a bastard, but beloved, child of math and music, as it were."

"That makes sense," Ingram says. "Musical notes are mathematical, aren't they?"

"Quite." In truth is it is, as far as Kian understands it, a subject of much debate and even violent discourse, about the artistry versus mathematicality of music. Kian tends to believe that rejecting either side is halving one's power. Most older clerics do, in fact; the discourse seems to be more common to necromancers under a century. Or at least the violence of it is; those who come to the conversation from an older perspective, at least on the British Isles, are primarily politely snide.

Kian picks out an appropriate pen and then considers the room again. The wards do not necessarily need to last forever, but he doesn't know how long he'll be here; and hotels tend to frown on people drawing on their walls. There are three framed pictures hanging: he takes them down, needing to smooth a shadow under one to make it unstick, and selects an appropriately-located corner as a fourth bearing; then places in corners just under carpet, and carefully drawing on the sides of window frames, where they are unlikely to ever be noticed.

Just bars: no notes. Yet. When he turns around Ingram is sipping her hot chocolate and frowning up at his work which will be concealed by one of the frames. "It's empty. What about the notes?"

"Those will be provided rather more literally," Kian answers, stoppering the ink and wiping off the pen, and placing them both carefully back in their case. He catches her still frowning, and adds: "It's transmission ink."

"Ah." Ingram's frown clears, and her face looks far more pleasant that way, now that the immediate danger has passed and fear no longer has permanent residence in her eyes. "I've never seen it used before."

"It can be sensitive," Kian acknowledges. "Some users can use a single ink for many purposes; but alas, I lack the talent and education in amalgamating transmitters in such a fashion." That's why he has many different inks.

"I thought necromancers work primarily in music."

"Oh, we do," Kian assures her, finding his violin case and setting it on the bed to open. "But Ireland has a long history of oral traditions combining music and storytelling; I find the crossover to be far less onerous than many others."

"It's impressive," Ingram says, and adds hastily when Kian looks at her with his most charming smile, the one which implies a witty response is imminent even though it is, in fact, not: "That is: music and stories can be considered separate disciplines in their own rights. To combine them, particularly when you already have a discipline, is impressive."

It still sounds an awful lot like she's saying *he's* impressive, but Kian merely laughs and lifts his violin. She isn't wrong; but disciplines shift, and in Ireland, at least, they had never been separate disciplines in truth. Such was the culture in which he'd been raised. The Irish church isn't the only such necromantic institution which uses them in such a fashion — particularly if the churches have managed to maintain their mature populations. In this case, it isn't a story he wants: or at least not one specific. He doesn't know Egypt well enough to provide a storied ward; and even if he did, Ireland is too full of tragically romantic heroes to be a shield against tragedy, unless he chooses to cast with vengeance in mind.

Kian doesn't particularly like vengeance, as a theme. It's far too *limiting*.

Ingram sits in one of the armchairs and says nothing as he prepares and deliberates, and Kian may or may not flaunt just a *touch*, just to give her an implication of a show rather than mundanity; and then he plays. The music of the akh had been mournful and long, full of lonely spaces and threads which were not present. Kian plays a jaunty folk dance from before Ireland had been conquered, from a time long before even his, but remembered in the steadfast patriotism of men and women such as his parents. It has none of the threads of wistful demand of *Let The People Sing*: it has none of the acknowledgement that Ireland might be a *conquered* island. It has nothing to suggest it *could* be conquered, let alone by lonely, half-there pieces of souls still fixated on their deaths.

In this, themes are important. Bright counters dreary, lively to counter mournful; everything the akh are *not*, are the wards. At the very least they will find it jarring, and the simple act of attempting to enter will warn the inhabitants that the tune has changed; at best, they'll find it simply unconscionable to be near, and will flee without Kian or Ingram needing to lift a finger. Kian is hoping for the latter: that the very existence of such music will pain them.

The room is filled with the scents of fresh meadows' grass and firelight, come with the hint of wood smoke; while burning isn't precisely Kian's preferred means, it's what this song likes in particular. When he visits the bars inked on the walls, his violin still resting on his aching shoulder, tune is engraved in notes on the walls with the precision of the finest laser, and only the faintest coil of smoke.

They'll last. He may be fined for defacing property, if anyone catches them before he leaves, but they're small scrolling things which could well be affectations the proprietors would like to keep.

For now, they fill the room with the faintest of chords; like a hum of electricity, invisible until it's silent and only then it feels apparent. The room seems fuller for it — but then, he prefers rooms to be full in this fashion. When he turns Ingram certainly looks pole-axed, if covering well; or this is how he chooses to interpret the expression on her face warring between wonder and closed clinical consideration. He bows, cheerful and a little sardonic. "I do hope you've enjoyed this taste of how my payments may be rendered, Healer Ingram."

His words could be taken for salacious, though he keeps his tone politely airy, and her expression morphs into something like exasperation; if not fond, then leaning toward amusement.

"If you've hurt your shoulder," she says, "I'll lecture you while you drink your hot chocolate. Have you?"

Kian lowers his violin into its case and rolls his shoulder carefully. It aches, but when he tests skin under shirt with his fingers, nothing has opened: new scar, still prone to pain beneath the surface, but nothing more. "I believe I shall survive, Healer Ingram."

"Good." She gets up to hand him his hot chocolate anyway, standing there until he takes it; and then she nods down at the violin. "Is that how you began?"

"After a fashion." Kian pats it with his spare hand. "I learned the violin as a child, though this isn't that one. It took me a significant amount of time to pick up a violin after the death of my parents." He speaks matter-of-factly. This, of all things, is perhaps a grudge he cannot forgive: but it's an old one, and there's no one on which to exact it, besides. There is now no other way to approach the matter. "In the church, acolytes learn all kinds of instruments — it's a tool of trade. We specialise, of course; but in a pinch, any of us can use any tool at our disposal."

Ingram nudges the case without quite laying hand on it. "What made you pick it up again?"

Kian smiles. "I was sent abroad for training and wound up in the Duchy of Milan. There was a luthier there with an innovative eye and a lust for craftmanship, and an insistent need to know the reason for my disdain. For science, you see; and for artistry. He felt that if he could win over a sceptic, he could win over anyone."

She waits a moment while he closes the lid, and then prompts: "Would I recognise the name of this luthier, if you said it?"

"Most likely," Kian answers, and returns the violin's case to the wall, within reach of the cot; and then he turns, mug still in hand. "Now, we have a choice to make, Healer Ingram. It has not been long since we slept, though it could perhaps do us well so soon after so much healing." He pauses at this last, with the faintest upturn of a question she answers with a nod. "Or we can go and investigate Canary Wharf, and see what he's left behind."

"If we left the room, the akh would come after us again, wouldn't they?"

"Most likely," Kian acknowledges. "We would be better prepared for their presence: I doubt they can hide the impact their presence has, and now we're aware of it, we're unlikely to be caught off-guard." He speaks without shame. Unreasoning fear is just that: unreasoning. It's galling and annoying, but hardly shameful. "We would need the protection of our friend at all times, however." He nods toward the skeleton.

"And if we waited?"

"It would be more time for Carruthers to continue his plans, or move his possessions — though it's likely there will be nothing left even now. On the other hand, akh would no doubt have more trouble moving in daylight, if only due to the presence of so many others and the need to be discreet."

"But it would be harder to investigate Canary Wharf in daylight," she says, and Kian inclines his head with agreement. There is a moment when her brow is furrowed, small and thoughtful, while the rim of her empty mug rests against her lip; and Kian attempts to keep his attention on her eyes, instead.

"You have a thought, Healer Ingram?"

"He provides a service, doesn't he? Couldn't we go there under the cover of being clients?"

"If he's there," Kian says, "it would certainly make things interesting. After all, even if he doesn't know our names and faces, he surely knows *us* by now."

"If he's there," Ingram points out coolly, "he can hardly make a fuss with so many offices in use on the floor."

Daring. Audacious. Oh, Kian likes her. Not only likes: respects. That is either a terrible combination, or quite the fun one, depending; for now, it's merely ... a combination. Kian smiles, and toasts her with a bow. "I do like the way you think, Healer Ingram. Then, tonight we rest; and tomorrow we beard a lion in its den."

EIGHTEEN

PULLING UP THE BIG-BOY PANTS

R est includes research, as far as Rosemary is concerned. She spends a little time looking into Carruthers's business to put together a cover story that will at least hold up past the first encounter. Mostly, the business appears to be about moving money politely and quietly from one place to another, and making sure it garners as much additional money in the process as possible. That would account for the bland occupation title, she supposes.

Her mind keeps drifting back to Kian and his violin, and the fascinating wonder of the work he's just done on the wards. Had they the time and luxury, she'd ask him to do it over a few times so she could observe fully.

Perhaps later, once someone is no longer trying to kill them. This concept is still a little surreal. Rosemary adjusts to it in bits and pieces as she goes about what night-time routines she can in this setting. The concierge was able to provide a charger for her phone, at least, and between that piece of usefulness and the hotel's provided toiletries, she feels as human as she ever does by the time she considers turning in.

"Is it worth arguing with you over who takes the cot?" Rosemary asks Kian thoughtfully, when he's glanced up from his tablet at her.

He has an array of smiles from charming to sarcastic; a number of them have edges in them. This one doesn't seem to, yet. "I really don't think it is, Healer Ingram," he says, as mannerly as ever. "I'm sufficiently comfortable there, and already set up accordingly."

Rosemary eyes him dubiously a moment longer, suspicious on principle. But: it's an upscale enough hotel that the quality can be expected to be correspondingly reasonable, and if he's already slept there and found nothing lacking then she suppose she has no justification left for argument.

Besides. She doesn't *really* want to give up the bed, once practicality has been factored in and taken care of.

She spares a few moments to check his injuries, which Kian graciously allows with only a little nagging. They're progressing sufficiently — Rosemary nudges the process just a touch anyway, since sleep is imminent, and lets go. "I'll want to look again in the morning," she reminds him.

"Of course, Healer Ingram."

He's far too tractable. Either she's misjudged him or he's plotting something.

But the night passes peaceably enough into morning, and Rosemary sleeps well and deeply. No dreams — she's expecting nightmares at one point or another, which almost makes it more irritating her subconscious isn't dredging up relics of the last few days for review.

Room-service provides breakfast. Rosemary takes advantage to check over Kian's injuries again. Within acceptable parameters — she's no longer worried he's going to tear something open again, only for his unimpeded function — and so she doesn't add further input, only makes a note of the progress and takes her awareness from him. "Everything looks good enough," she reports briskly. "Not perfect, but not at immediate risk. Any lingering pain?"

Kian tests his shoulder carefully, then the way his injured leg takes his weight. "Some aches, but nothing serious," he says. "I appreciate your efforts, Healer Ingram."

It's a form of self-interest, really, especially since she still has a notion that she's getting paid if they both live through this. Rosemary holds her tongue on that. "Don't take it as license to be careless," she says sharply, and goes to get dressed.

Her clothes from two nights ago are still tolerably clean, but it's starting to irritate her, having *nothing* else. She hasn't been back yet, to the clinic and her flat above to see what might be left, but surely anything left will have smoke so ingrained it will take magical intervention to save, if any is even possible in the first place. Better to write off now, make a cleaner cut so any remnants are an unlooked-for hope.

So: nothing. She still has the bank card in her phone case, at least, so that's a start; she can pick up a couple of things today, and no doubt should, if they're attempting to look ambiguously moneyed. There's still some time pressure, naturally, but it feels less during the day. Safer, perhaps, where fragmented ghosts have a harder time reaching.

Kian is unfailingly polite as their morning ablutions stumble around each other. Somehow it makes Rosemary feel rather more of an obstruction, but this, too, she puts away, and bulls on ahead anyway, since there is little other option.

There's a knock at the door as they're readying to go. Helpful timing, at least. Rosemary glances back at Kian, wondering — but no, a knock is a knock, and the faint distant hum of the wards remains in a state that passes for quiescent, and Kian doesn't appear too very concerned.

The visitor proves to be the police. Rosemary thinks it's one of those they spoke to outside her clinic, but she can't honestly tell. Kian treats the man as though they've met before, at least, which is cue enough. "How can we help you, Constable?"

There's an awkward glance around the room, and the constable moves further in when invited, offers photos. They've tracked down the car Kian reported as having tried to run him down, and neighbouring security footage confirms. They haven't managed to arrest the driver, only locate the car, but they managed to get a usable picture off the cameras, and does Kian recognize this man? Or does Rosemary?

She peers dutifully, but is sure even before she gets a look that she won't. It was before Kian's troubles came to her as well, and sure enough, the face doesn't ring a bell for her, even with the clarity of the night-time image refined and filtered as it obviously has been. She shakes her head, apologetic, and steps out of the conversation

167

while Kian and the constable confer further. Kian wants a copy of the picture, it sounds like, and the constable doesn't particularly think he should be allowed to walk off with evidence.

While the constable is probably correct, Rosemary wouldn't bet on him winning. She occupies herself getting ready to go instead, while Kian negotiates a compromise involving taking a picture of the picture, so that no evidence actually *leaves* police hands.

"A face is better than I had hoped," Kian says once he's managed to disengage from the conversation and close the door. He's studying the picture on his own phone now, turning it this way and that as though looking at the face upside-down will help. It's not a very remarkable face, Rosemary had noted. Male, white or close enough to it that he looks pale in the washed-out lighting, short hair. Nondescript, on the whole.

"You have no idea who he is," Rosemary says, though surely Kian doesn't need her to point that out.

He waves a hand as if this isn't actually an issue at all. "A picture is better than a vague description or none at all. There's the license plate, too. I have at least one contact who can follow this up."

It's probably going to approach the point of technomancy where Rosemary isn't sure she wants to know the details. Certainly there are going to be large breaches of privacy — but then again, this man did try to help murder Kian.

Kian spends some little further time over that, and then he, too, is prepared to go, and they start for the door; and then the skeleton, which has been quietly observing in its corner, starts to its feet to go with them. Rosemary draws her breath in sharp, startled by its existence again — people really can get used to anything, can't they?

"Of course," Kian says, resigned. "We should at least pull the hood up."

Rosemary appears to have been volunteered for this duty, judging by how Kian doesn't move. She closes with the skeleton, and it moves only twice: to turn its head to watch her, and to put a hand up to the hood. It seems a tentative kind of gesture, Rosemary thinks. "Yes," she says, as if instructing, and briskly flips the hood over the bare skull. "The hood."

When she turns toward the door again Kian is wearing a faint frown as he studies the two of them, and his fingers drum one quick roll on the handle of his cane. "— Let's be off, then," he says abruptly, and finally, finally they get moving.

Outside the room Rosemary becomes aware of a strange quality to the air; and it takes until they are nearly out onto the street before she can place it as an *absence* of sound, some low hum or pressure from Kian's wards that so thoroughly slipped into her consciousness that she stopped noticing it until it was gone. It's good craftsmanship, she supposes, it's just going to take a moment or two to adjust every time they have to go in or out.

Still better than having to contend with the akh, and the fear they had brought with them.

"We'll need to stop for clothing," she says briskly, already pulling up a map to run a quick search for nearby clothing shops that will be more useful than the average trendy, high-priced boutique. "Ideally, some basic business-wear for me, and ... well." She casts a glance back at their skeleton-shadow. Knowing the soul-reaver is a solid weight in its front pocket is both reassurance and concern. "We might find something less conspicuous for our friend."

"I don't think that would be especially difficult," Kian says dryly.

Rosemary knows without shadow of a doubt he is judging the bright yellow wellies. In her defence, they were donated.

There's a shopping centre directly on Canary Wharf, it transpires, and while the thought of the pricing makes Rosemary wince, the trade-off for not being out and about longer than strictly necessary might be worth it. She's not trying to replenish an entire wardrobe here, after all, only acquire two outfits. Possibly less than that, depending what can be kept.

And also the fact that there is no version of this shopping trip in which Rosemary possibly wants to purchase underwear with Kian accompanying her.

So it's a taxi, then, with the skeleton between them, and Rosemary uncomfortably aware of the points of its hipbones digging against hers whenever there's too sharp a turn. It keeps its head down as instructed, mercifully, and the cab driver doesn't seem to want to look too closely, which is also a relief.

They're let out a little ways from their destination, which is a compromise between Kian's desire for subtlety and Rosemary's preference for him still not walking long distances. From there it's a terribly slow progress of window-shopping, assessing and discarding shop possibilities as suiting their needs. Kian has significantly more discernment than Rosemary, and he rejects a few options out of hand — "The quality is obviously subpar, anyone who knows what they're looking at will peg you for playing dress-up."

"Maybe that's for the best," Rosemary says at this one, thoughtfully. "If we say I am recently come into a surprising inheritance and looking to invest, then it would stand to reason I would be somewhat naïve about the handling of money, and probably inexperienced in matters of quality fashion, to boot."

Kian looks, so faintly Rosemary is half-convinced she imagined it, pained at this logic. He does not immediately argue with her, which Rosemary takes as license to go inside and start hunting.

It's immediately clear they're not going to be able to get away with anything fitted on the skeleton. Oversized is better. It would be better still if they could concoct some sort of frame to at least pretend it has human musculature, but they don't have time for that sort of craftsmanship. Sweats it is, though they can at least find something more uniform.

Rosemary hunts for something approximating a suit, though firmly draws the line at anything involving a skirt. It might be the more accepted thing fashionably, but there's a higher chance than she'd like that she'll have to run from someone or something in these clothes. Pants. Good slacks which can be paired with nearly anything, a dress shirt — she considers white, remembers she barely has any contrast to her to begin with, and settles on blue. There's a vague, wistful thought for a waistcoat, but the shop doesn't have any tailored for women, and she'd really rather not outright mirror Kian.

A scarf instead, then, long and draping, and she defers to Kian's judgment on colour here, winds up with a white one instead of the orange she was half-tempted by. "Please don't," he says, shaking his head at the shade, and while Rosemary will absolutely keep it in mind for later, she will concede that sticking out is the opposite of what they want to do.

She keeps her clogs, worn as they are.

Rosemary does a quick check of the dressing-rooms for security cameras before she tries to get anything on the skeleton. The size is eyeballed, the clothing pre-purchased — nothing fancy, only darker, matching sweats, and a scarf to pull up over its face. Cheap sneakers. It's a small mercy it's not the dead of summer.

Cameras in the hall, but not in the rooms, which results in Rosemary motioning the skeleton into the largest of the rooms, and briskly beginning to strip the current clothing off it. It doesn't give her much argument, but it isn't helping either, and Rosemary begins to think she needs at least three hands to get it to do what she needs. "Putting on pants is not *that* hard," she informs it with some frustration, arranging the new sweatpants on the floor for the third time after she's failed to get its feet in place. "You can do it."

It regards her with blank light in its eye-sockets.

Rosemary huffs, and leans out of the room. "Kian, I need your hands, please."

Kian raises an eyebrow at her. Rosemary narrows her eyes. He opts to comply without anything overly charming, coming off the wall and crossing over to her. "Oh, very well. What may I hold for you, Healer Ingram?"

"Bones," she says crossly, and turns around just in time to see the skeleton pull the sweatpants up. "There — if you could do that all along, why didn't you?" This is a more severe demand. Rosemary moves on with business anyway, tamping down the irritation as she goes for the hoodie. "Arms up, please."

It complies, more or less, even if it isn't aiming very well. Rosemary manages to navigate the hoodie, though she's getting rather less help than she thought she might have. When she glances back, Kian is still, and staring intently. "Kian?" she says, to get his attention.

He shakes his head as if to clear it, focuses on her instead of past her. "Are you sure you need my help? You managed deftly enough last time."

"Last time it wasn't shuffling this much." It's settled now, though, and Rosemary tugs the hood up. This one is bigger in the hood, hides the skull better. "There. Good enough at a casual glance."

Kian says nothing for some time. "Yes," he concurs finally. "Good enough for now."

"Then we should go," Rosemary says, and, "Whatever you're not saying, I'd like to know about it later." It's a shot in the dark, but the way Kian inclines his head says there is something.

"Let's be off," he agrees, and she collects her things and their skeleton, heads after him. Next stop, the lion's den, as it were. It'll almost be a relief to get it over and done with.

NINETEEN

KNOW YOUR ENEMY

Canary Wharf is far livelier at this time of morning, and this time Kian minds it far less, being appropriately dressed. The skeleton is still a factor, but at least in this case it isn't Gregory, nor with Gregory's urgent need to be reunited with his body. All this skeleton seems to desire is to watch them. Closely. Kian is not ordinarily unnerved by the regard of the undead, but in this case his back prickles.

It had pulled up its own pants. It did not have a brain; it hadn't even had one temporarily, while Gregory inhabited it. There's no possible way it could have *learned how to dress itself* — and yet. Even reanimations *with* brains find it difficult to learn new things. And yet.

It's the soul-reaver. It has to be. Kian had gone through the materials provided by the archivist a second time, but they had been about the soul-reavers owned rather than soul-reavers themselves. He regrets, now, not having asked for more general information; he does not at all recall any rumours about soul-reavers being *alive* in any sense. Then again, he has to wonder how many people are stupid, or desperate, enough to forge a blood-bond with it. It had seemed logical at the time; blood is not, after all, a lasting binding agent.

Kian attempts not to brood about this on their way to the appropriate tower, but it's still forefront in his mind as they find the elevator and ascend. They aren't alone in the elevator and so there's no opportunity to discuss their story further; Kian hums idly, watching the numbers tick up, and when they exit he holds the door for Ingram and ushers her out like the perfect gentleman he is. The halls look precisely the same they had previously, save that there's other people in them. It's fortunate they'd spoken at the dressing-rooms, the only likely quiet place at their disposal. It's fortunate, also, that Ingram is quite the pragmatic woman, because it means Kian had not had to convince her of much.

Pragmatic does not mean accustomed to undercover, nor potentially confronting a man who has attempted now to kill them multiple times. Ingram's breathing is active, like someone having to consciously focus on it, and when Kian glances down he sees her fingers trembling.

"Ms Ingram." Kian speaks quietly and waits until she glances up, and yes, her pupils are dilated. Kian gives her his most charming smile and holds out his arm, and she stares at it for a moment before she realises he means for her to take it, and does. Perfectly ordinary couple here, yes. At least this will hide the tremor in her hands, and give her something on which to steady himself. Hopefully the more overt signs of fear will be lessened, because Carruthers almost certainly knows them.

"How do you cope?" she murmurs while their heads are bent toward each other, just slightly.

"I'm hardly young anymore," Kian answers dryly, "and this isn't the first time I've risked confronting someone in ... similar circumstances, shall we say."

"I'm going to ask you about those other times, on a later occasion," Ingram says, sounding amused and reserved at once.

"Ms Ingram, I'm flattered. That surely sounds like you intend to see me after I've paid my invoice."

"Oh, honestly," she mutters, but she seems less tense, which is precisely what Kian had intended. She still clutches his arm a little tighter than strictly necessary, but Kian forbears under the circumstances, and in only a short period of time they come to the area where Carruthers's office had been. In the darkness of early morning it had been difficult to distinguish precise layout; now with daylight and people, it proves that Carruthers's office uses the same receptionist as a cluster of others, cordoned by a desk they had bypassed in the darkness their first visit. Fortunately Carruthers's website had indicated walk-ins were accepted, so there should be no need to pretend after missing appointments.

Kian draws his attention by tapping the edge of the desk with his cane-handle until the receptionist looks up with a smile. "How can I help you?"

"We've a need to see Mr Carruthers," Kian says. "Is he in quite yet? We *are* early." He sounds appropriately apologetic, and certainly the receptionist sees nothing untoward, at least in part because Ingram's on his far side, and thus the whiteness of her knuckles aren't immediately visible.

"He's just stepped out to get a coffee," says the receptionist, and points them to the door they have already been through once. "Go on and wait for him in his office; he shouldn't be long, he just likes the coffee at the bottom of the tower."

Kian bows a little, and Ingram nods stiffly, and they head on down the hall. "That's a piece of luck," he murmurs, "but not much time."

"Enough to see inside the wall," Ingram murmurs back, "provided you're correct about where the door is."

"I have every confidence in myself," Kian answers blithely, and opens the door for Ingram with a little bow to usher her inside. She takes a breath and lifts her chin and enters like a woman with self-assurance feeling out of place — which is, really, the truth as well as being their cover. Ingram has come into some money unexpectedly: Kian is her lawyer. He is hardly conventionally educated, but his unique position and several centuries means he is eminently familiar with laws, how they work, and how they've changed. Carruthers, of course, is up to twice Kian's age and thus with more experience; but there's a certain point where the years plateau and no longer serve as an adequate barometer for whom might hoodwink whom.

(This is an assertion in which Kian is fairly confident, seeing as one Cleric Cabhan ó Cuinn of the Irish Church still hasn't figured out why unpleasant objects keep appearing in his clothes bureau, despite this having been a regular occurrence whenever he's a particular arsehole since they were acolytes. Age, in that case, has not at all wisened.)

The office is empty when they enter and Kian closes the door behind them, save a plastic runner on the floor where Kian's blood had been frozen into the carpet and the fact that the desk and chairs have been shifted a few feet to the side in order to avoid it. If he didn't know the cause of the move, he would not have thought it was a forced shift, but simply the chosen layout. Certainly, Carruthers has a sense of class — at least, the sort in which everything has the appearance of being deliberate.

They take but a moment to take in the room, and then Ingram goes to the desk, while Kian heads for the bookcases. From the desk, it's easier for Ingram to sit down in a hurry if they hear anyone approach; and Kian has enough knowledge and gumption to bluff being near the books.

"The drawers are locked again," Ingram announces, and moves around the desk to look at the open laptop while Kian runs his fingers along the seam of the cases. The freezer had been near the end furthest from the door, so he works his way back, looking for evidence of a doorway. "So is the laptop."

"A pity," Kian murmurs, but to be expected. Laptops are easily locked, if one gets in the habit whenever they stand.

"Will you come and unlock the drawer?"

"It's unlikely he's put the knives there," Kian says without looking around. "He already knows the lock is no deterrent. Check the papers on the desk, if any." Here; the dust is disturbed, however light the layer had been to begin with. And — he peers closer — yes, there it is: a little groove on the inside of the shelf, like a handle. Kian pulls out the book on the end so he can fit his hand in, and it takes some groping before he squints into the gap. It was there. He was sure of it. It was — what was it?

"Kian?" Kian shakes his head hard and looks around, blinking, at Ingram. She stands by the desk, still close to the chairs in the event of footsteps, and looks at him with a frown. "You were standing there."

"What are we looking for?" he asks, feeling fuzzy and frazzled and as if there's something on the tip of his tongue.

"A door," Ingram answers, and her frown deepens. "We're looking for a door in the wall, to see what he's keeping in the space between offices."

"Ah." Yes. That's right; he does remember that. He remembers, primarily, feeling very annoyed with himself for not realising there *would* be a room, when he'd even noted that there was a significant amount of space between. Somehow he hadn't put it together. 'Somehow.' "There is most definitely a forget-me ward on this stretch of bookcases."

Ingram's frown clears to contemplative understanding. "I see. That's why we didn't think of it while we were here last."

"Indeed," says Kian dryly, and does not dare turn around as he reaches between books, groping without sight. "It's a subtle one that didn't stand up against obstinacy where the freezer was concerned, but it seems there's another under it."

He's not thinking of the shallow grip he's looking for. He's not thinking about opening doors. He's not thinking about *searching*, and thus his fingers brush against a mismatch in texture, and curl in, and he feels something depress and the balance of the bookcase shift with a near-silent clunk between timber. This, surely, would have taken some money and some attention. Few people need secret rooms in their rented offices.

Kian steps back to give the door room to swing, wary of touching the inside jamb now that wards are clear. It's entirely possible they've set off something else; but Kian is no wardbreaker, nor all that accomplished at divining their presence besides through the use of logic. All he can do, really, is be aware of traps and step in. So far, he's managed.

"What are you waiting for?" Ingram asks after he's stood contemplating the door for a few additional seconds, tapping the handle of his cane.

"Merely trying to determine what other wards might be present," Kian answers absently. The door is narrow, and the room inside cool even from standing outside it; the threshold is a clean line between carpet and concrete. There's no marks he can see on the walls or inside jamb, and when he smooths the edge of the carpet with his toe it doesn't pull up, nor is there evidence of it having been nailed or drilled down. Unlikely to be written wards under it, then.

If there are any further wards than that, they're going to be ones Kian doesn't know how to circumvent. And there's nothing to see from the outside: simple bare concrete and steel pylons, like the frame of a room not meant to be seen. If there's anything else in there, he shall have to step in; and he doesn't believe, knowing the kinds of wards Carruthers has used thus far, that it would be strictly dangerous — at or least not *violent*.

So he does, and immediately the space is disorienting, like the room has flipped and there's crushing weight overhead, evident owing to its looming presence rather than any sight of it; he feels as though he's stepped underground, into a tomb musty with stone and sand, cool despite that there ought to be heat from the sands outside —

"Kian?"

He turns and stares blankly, and there's nothing over the threshold of the tomb, nothing but sand and sun and pounding heat. Where had that voice come from? Who was that?

Had that been his name they'd called?

"*Kian.*"

He looks around the narrow space and grips his cane, knuckles white. It's cool in here but hot out there, and neither temperature is what makes him break out in a cold sweat. He can't *tell* what makes him break out into a cold sweat, except that heat means death and the cold yawning passage leads to a tomb; and so he stands paralysed, not sure which way to turn or even, indeed, who he is.

Then comes the song: first a hum, then something scattered, words connected by the la-la-la of someone who isn't sure of lyrics; but it's familiar, tugging at his heart like a physical thing. His lips move, filling in gaps with words he knows but doesn't; and all at once the tomb is *weight*, the space is much much smaller, and he is aware enough of being enclosed in something terribly malicious in its ability to strip identity. At the threshold there's a woman, just beyond in the sunlight, and she beckons him with hand and with half-known song, and suddenly the heat of sand seems far preferable to the cold.

Moving over the threshold is instead like going from stiflingly hot to blessedly cold water, and Kian gasps for the relief of it, staggering with hand out. Ingram is the one who catches him, steadying him until he stops shaking and takes a deeper, more steadying breath.

"Don't enter," he says, perhaps unnecessarily, and rather dizzied.

"I gathered," Ingram says, dry even by his standards, and guides him to one of the chairs. "Another ward?"

"A powerful one," Kian murmurs, and submits to being nudged to sit, and takes another deep, calming breath. That had been — oddly terrifying, and in a fashion different from the akh. "Close the door."

Ingram nods and goes to close the bookcase. "Could you see anything?"

"No. Not even peering. If there's anything in there, it's squarely around the corner." Kian shakes his head, resting his hands on his cane, on the floor. "There may be, still — since the ward lingers."

"What kind was it?" Ingram asks, coming back to the chairs and taking a seat, folding her hands over her lap as if they're having a perfectly ordinary conversation in a perfectly ordinary office.

"It was a forgetting ward," Kian says slowly, "of a kind I've never met before. It wasn't simply forgetting what I was doing: it was forgetting *me*. It felt as if it was trying to erase me from existence." He glances up to look at her, and manages a small smile he knows is not up to par, but is all he can manage. "I appreciate your insight and intelligence, Healer Ingram. You did precisely the right thing."

"It was the only thing that made sense," Ingram answers. "You said you use it to form bindings."

"And yet, not everyone is quite so logical about such conclusions," Kian answers dryly, and glances around. The office seems perfectly ordinarily boring, and yet: now he's aware of it, he can't help but think of that desire to see foes *erased*. His experience with Egyptian beliefs is still limited, but he's read enough to know some concepts about names and the significance thereof in their afterlife. The greatest revenge, surely, is being forgotten. He suppresses a shiver and rises. "Well. If we can't enter, there's no point in lingering. At the very least, we are told he intends to be here for some period still."

"Very well," Ingram agrees, and rises also; and naturally it's then as they turn that the door opens and Carruthers is framed in the exit.

TWENTY

CAUTIOUS CONSULTATIONS

Too late to leave. Now there is only what's before them, and Rosemary pays very close attention to the situation at hand. Mr Timothy Carruthers certainly doesn't look like he has ancient Egyptian sorcery and a taste for cruelty in the shadows. He looks like he might have been very handsome twenty years ago; he has the look of a vintage movie heart-throb, gone silver about the crown and stern about the mouth. There are lines at the corners of his eyes, creases where he has frowned too long and too hard, but his skin is the sort of pale that has rarely seen prolonged sun. "Ah," he says, glancing from Rosemary to Kian. "The walk-ins. What can I do for you?"

Rosemary is more grateful than ever that they had those moments of exchange to at least lay down the bare bones of a cover-story. She would still rather not be here now, of course, but it's better than nothing at all. "A consultation," she says. She doesn't have the luxury of panic. "If you have the time, of course. I've recently come into some money, and I'd like to be intelligent about my investments."

"Of course," he says. There's something about his tone, even in so few words, that makes Rosemary feel *indulged* rather than acknowledged, and she can't say she much likes it. Carruthers offers a short bow rather than a handshake, just antique enough to be charming. "As you may have surmised, I am Timothy Carruthers. And you are?" This last as he moves around his desk to take up his chair.

Rosemary knows she put things back just in the same positions they were, but nevertheless her heart jumps with the uncertainty, the fear that they may somehow be caught out anyway. "Heather," she says, casts about for a suitable surname, and adds, "Heather Chandler. A pleasure to meet you." She's going to be watching her words very carefully.

Carruthers turns an inquiring glance toward Kian, and mercifully Kian is by now self-possessed enough to answer readily. "Kian Ó Maolomhnaigh," he says, with a pleasant little smile of his own. "I'm a friend of the family."

"Irish, I perceive," Carruthers says, and there's something else there, some additional weight as Carruthers looks him over. Rosemary is certainly missing some layer of dynamic, she thinks, somewhere between the insincere smiles being traded. "It has a rhythm to it."

"I've always rather thought so," Kian agrees, in the bright tone of cheerful nothings.

"And your friend?" Carruthers follows up, and he doesn't take his eyes off Kian, but inclines his head to the corner where the skeleton is lingering.

Rosemary feels vaguely slighted and vaguely concerned in quick succession. She had hoped he would overlook the skeleton. But Kian has a story, or something like it, and is answering before Rosemary has the chance to worry so very much. "My cousin," Kian says smoothly. "... Connor. Please don't worry about him; he's mostly here so he wouldn't be home alone."

Carruthers looks, by Rosemary's estimation, very sceptical. "I see," he says delicately, with lightly raised eyebrows, and Rosemary is for a moment completely, terribly certain that he hasn't bought the off-the-cuff story. But he says nothing more of it, and lets it pass, and Rosemary relaxes just a touch. It may not be much, but at least this one thing isn't something that needs to be worried about *right* now. "Well. Any detailed advice, of course, will be put off until after we have signed a contract and my fee is arranged, but I can certainly give you an idea of what to expect and what I can do for you. Did you have specific ideas?"

She had absolutely none. Rosemary shakes her head, takes a moment to think back, to find something like a parallel in her history. It isn't perfect — it was years and years ago that she and Rowan were expelled from elfin lands, and a bribe to cut ties is hardly an inheritance — but she remembers at least the feeling of being uncertain and overwhelmed, and nevertheless determined to do things as correctly as possible. "Some is earmarked for schooling, and so on," she says, "but besides that, there's still nearly a hundred-thousand to work with, and quite frankly I barely know where to start. What would you recommend? Broadly, of course."

"Let me show you a sample portfolio," Carruthers says, and turns to his computer. "Generic, but it will give you an idea of how I like to do things."

"I appreciate it," Rosemary murmurs. The interlude that follows is full of a nervous tension, at least on her part — there is the click of keys and the hum of the computer's fan, and every sound seems twice the volume it should be, but if she volunteers conversation the odds of tripping up grow steadily larger.

Kian does not seem to have gotten that memo. He leans forward, still cheerful-bright, the head of his cane clacking as it settles against the deck. "So," he says, "Timothy — Tim?"

"Timothy," Carruthers says, absently unamused.

"Timothy," Kian concedes. "Very well. How long have you been in this business, may I ask?"

Of course the man is not going to tell them *'several hundred years'*. Does Kian just feel it his responsibility to poke and prod at everyone?

"Here, thirteen years." Carruthers taps a few more buttons. "Before this, I travelled for a while; but we all have to settle down sometime, don't we? And I've always loved how the numbers flow."

"How lovely. Where did you travel?" Kian inquires. If he says anything about Egypt, Rosemary may be forced to do something drastic to silence him. There is careful inquiry and then there is waving a damned red flag.

"A little bit of everywhere, really," Carruthers says, with the distant air of someone doing two things at once. Or, perhaps, someone evading specifics. "One moment." He stands then, goes to the door, and the receptionist from earlier meets him there, papers in hand. He takes them from him with a polite nod, during which exchange Rosemary finds the time to shoot Kian what she hopes is a meaningful look.

Kian taps one finger to his lips in response, either to communicate that he has a secret, or possibly that she should stop worrying. Neither of these options precisely reassure.

Carruthers returns and sits down, and spreads what looks initially like a dizzying array of numbers across the desk in front of Rosemary. "As you can see," he says, "I favour fairly diversified investments. Less risky, but of course you'll see more gradual returns rather than any one large lump sum. For security, it's a better approach." As Rosemary eyeballs what he has laid out, she makes better sense of it — he shows a little here, a little there, investments in companies indicated by placeholder text rather than actual names. Different industries, different returns. It's a mock-up, nothing more; nothing she could take to the bank, as it were.

The logic, though, is there. "I think I see," Rosemary says, to fill the space. "And I assume your fee is figured — somewhere?"

"A percentage," he says, turning over the page to indicate a space on the next. There's a flat number based on the round estimates he has made up, labelled with the equation to the left. "To bind our successes together, as it were. It only seems fair."

"How very equitable," Kian murmurs. Rosemary wishes he wouldn't make love to the word equitable.

"I strive to please," Carruthers says blithely. "Well. I'll give you this, and — ah, here. A sample contract based on my standard terms." Another sheet of paper tucked under the others, and he reaches briefly into a drawer to pull out a folder of heavy, high-quality cardstock, tucks the papers into it. "My card, as well. I'll be able to plan more specifically once you've decided to commit, Ms Chandler."

For a moment Rosemary can't think who Ms Chandler is. A little belatedly she remembers her assumed surname. "That seems reasonable," she says distantly. "I'm afraid I'm rather out of my depth here, so I do appreciate your patience."

"After all, I'd hardly get much business if I chased the neophytes out of my office for not knowing." Carruthers smiles at her, the stern lines smoothing to something more softly handsome. Rosemary returns something smaller, half-hearted. She still can't honestly tell how much he's noticed, how genuine he's being. How much of his eyes flicking to the side is for Kian, and how much is for the disguised skeleton. "Well. Do you have any questions for me?"

Rosemary goes blank. She should have questions, if she were truly an intelligent, curious potential investor. She has none. She wants to get them all out of there as soon as possible, but bolting will look even more suspicious. "I'm afraid I barely know what to ask," she demurs, spreading one hand flat over the folder and tugging it back toward her. "This was a little spur of the moment — I don't even have any of my own papers with me."

Kian leans forward, one elbow braced on the desk and his chin in his hand. "Ever been to Ireland?" he asks, making it sound like only polite wondering. "You sounded as though you might be familiar with the language."

Carruthers turns his eyes on Kian, and there's a look very like that from earlier, something with an assessing weight Rosemary can't quite put a name on. He says something, then, something long and liquid which has the sound of familiarity, somehow, though she can't pick the individual words out of it. Kian responds in kind, smooth and smiling, and Rosemary rather thinks his tone is mischievous.

"I have your card, if I have questions," Rosemary says, before they can go back and forth again, before Kian can over-play his hand as he seems to have been trying to do. "I do appreciate you taking the time."

"It's a pleasure," Carruthers says. He stands when she does, once more offers a bow instead of a handshake. "I look forward to hearing from you. Ms Chandler. ... Kian."

Rosemary decides, rather definitively, that she absolutely does not like his tone on that last.

"I'm sure," Kian says, rising with a distinctly ironic sweep of his hand, and a dip of his head in more or less reciprocal farewell.

Enough is enough. At this point, Rosemary doesn't care if it looks like they're rushing. "Connor," she says to the skeleton, and it turns toward her. "Come on. Kian?"

"Coming." Kian offers her his arm again, and Rosemary takes it, pleased to find she isn't so shaky as she was. All the same, she isn't so assured that she'll pass up a friendly hand, at the moment.

All the way out to the reception, Rosemary feels watched, and it's more than just the shuffling footsteps and ever-present existence of the skeleton behind her. It's a weight on the nape of her neck, the prickling along her spine, that tells her she is seen, and she honestly can't say how much to ascribe to intuition and how much to sheer nerves. All together, the whole thing can't have taken more than an hour; the conversation, surely not more than a quarter of that. And yet, she's as worn as if it had been half a day.

She doesn't say anything at all until Kian has bid the receptionist farewell, and the three of them are out to the street again. Here the air is fresh, the breeze brisk enough to stir her hair, and Rosemary draws deep breaths. She isn't going to let herself sit and shake until later, but the breathing is steadying.

"Let's move along, shall we?" Kian suggests. He's retained that bright, sharp-edged cheer, which is no small relief to see after how unlike himself he'd been, directly after the forgetting trap.

They haven't learned as much as she might like, but they're certainly not going to learn anything additional standing here. Rosemary nods carefully. She checks on the skeleton again — attentive, with them, knife still hidden — and then she moves on, keeping pace with Kian. "And when we're back at the hotel, you can tell me exactly what you thought you were doing," she says under her breath, as politely as she knows how.

"Of course, Healer Ingram." The smile is heard, even if it's not seen.

Rosemary forgets to let go of his arm for another several blocks, and Kian does her the courtesy of not commenting on it.

TWENTY-ONE

FOLLOW-UPS AND LET-DOWNS

They return to the Chamberlain not precisely leisurely, but without any further diversions. Ingram must surely require some additional ... specific ... clothes by now, and when Kian suggests, delicately, that she might like to do some additional shopping without him, he is quite intrigued to notice her ears shade red first — what he can see of them, when her hair is tied just so as to hide their tips. She is dignified about her refusal, if nothing else, and Kian does not press; he rather suspects she wants to grill him about some of his undercover choices before she can think about anything else. There is still plenty of the day left.

As expected, almost the moment the door is closed, Ingram wants answers. She does not, to be fair, whirl on him; she isn't nearly so uncontrolled. But she does turn and fix him with a baleful eye as Kian goes to one of the chairs and the coffee-table, where his tablet is sitting.

"What," she asks with dignified asperity, "were you thinking?"

Kian raises his eyebrow without sitting down to swipe for his emails. "To what instance, precisely, are you referring?"

"You gave him your name, to begin with," she answers in that tone he is beginning to recognise as preceding a lecture, and Kian can't help but laugh.

"I've not once come across someone *actually* capable of controlling names," he tells her, looking up with a smile and a little bow. "Present lineage excepted, of course." Since she's here, and only part-blooded, it's easy to guess that she was run out of elfin lands: the details for which he is not, of course, going to ask, since it's bound to be painful. Even the reminder makes her face tighten. "I realise from your perspective it must seem unbelievably reckless, but it isn't so common hereabouts, and if he knows who I am, and is at all likely to come for or send someone for me, then I will be ready."

"So you gave him your name as a trap," she notes, sounding displeased.

"No more a trap than walking directly into his office," Kian says mildly, but still with a charming smile, and Ingram grimaces.

"... That's true, I suppose. At least if he does come with you it will be on your terms. But don't you have a date tonight?"

"I do, and I find it unlikely he'll do anything noteworthy in a very public restaurant even if he somehow finds me *there*. It's more likely they'll come here." Kian glances toward 'Connor', whose name he had not *entirely* chosen before he'd spoken it, and whose syllables had resonated on his tongue like a half-there song he hadn't realised was stuck in his head. "For that reason, I'm going to insist our friend remains here with you while I seek out information."

For a moment Ingram looks as though she intends to argue, and then nods shortly, and with resignation. "I suppose he — *it* — would be too obvious in a crowded restaurant, not eating."

"Precisely." Kian looks down to his tablet. Verna still hasn't replied. Well, she does need to sleep — presumably. He's never met her in person, and thus really doesn't know whether she's fully human. Or in need of sleep. Occasionally he does wonder about the side-effects of technomancy. He looks up again, attentive to avoid giving the impression that he's being dismissive, which is not his intent. "Is there anything else about which you desired to lecture?"

Ingram's eyes narrow at him, and she crosses her arms. "Why were you flirting?"

Oh, is that all? "Because he gave me a look when I introduced myself," Kian answered with amusement, "and a bit of charm can result in deflection — and, if fortunate, an expedient escape. You were a bit nervous, Healer Ingram. I hoped to draw his attention. I believe it worked." She does not look at all happy, so Kian smiles as sunnily as he knows how, putting down the tablet. "Shall I order some tea?"

She gives him the dirtiest look he's seen from her yet, but acquiesces; and the next few hours are startlingly domestic. Kian does some reading. Some preparations for his date. Ensures he has the questions he desires to ask. In the end Ingram does, in fact, depart to do some additional shopping, glancing at him as she goes to the door. Kian does not miss the shade of her skin this time either, though she holds her head high; and the skeleton, silent as it hadn't been in those awful wellies, follows.

Kian spends the time while she's gone putting his thoughts in order. In the first place, the fact that the office is still warded is ... *intriguing*; either Carruthers considers himself just that safe or he expected them to return to try and find more. He is not entirely wrong in either case, though Kian is chagrined to admit it. He is, at least, alive to be chagrined; and this he counts as a victory.

Other than that: No location, *yet*; but he sends the picture the constable had allowed him, both to Verna and to a witch he knows in the area. At this late stage it's unlikely he'll be able to tell Kian much, as at this point the man in the car seems an unnecessary pursuit — and yet. Kian doesn't like loose ends. They have a way of tangling the larger thread.

The list of targets is still outstanding. Kian intends to show his date the man from the car — he was, Kian suspects, who had picked up the body. Verna had, at least, sent through a list of people in London in the lightning and metallurgist communities; it's a list of names to ask his date about also. Then he sets about preparing, at least as far as not to present himself as a total cad, though he certainly doesn't intend to go so far as to imply he would like a second date.

Ingram and her shadow return as he's pulling on his coat, and she gives him a studying look as she turns to put the bag down on the bed, conveniently hidden by her body. "You'll be off soon, then?"

"Quite," Kian agrees, and points to his tablet. "I've unlocked the tablet and turned on the email notifs. Verna has the associated number, so if she calls or emails, please feel free to answer or read. The longer we spend working on this, individually, the more information we shall hopefully be able to bring to one another when I return. Naturally, feel free to call for something dire; and in a pinch, the address is written on the notepad on the bureau."

"That seems logical," Ingram agrees calmly, and though Kian can't say she'd precisely lost her good humour before she left, she seems to have regained whatever of it there is to regain. "When should I expect your return?"

Kian checks his pocketwatch. "Well. We're scheduled for six, and unless she has vital information which warrants a second dinner, I shan't be planning on leading her on. So, perhaps eight-thirty, accounting for travel time."

Ingram stares at him for a moment with edges of bafflement and incredulity. "Do you," she asks carefully, "frequently lead women on?"

"No more than the men," Kian says cheerfully, and watches the blush descend under loosely bound hair, along lobes. "My dear Healer Ingram, do you believe sex is a tool only available to women? Dear me."

The blush takes a hard turn sideways to climb across her cheeks, and she clears her throat. "Is that ever necessary?"

Necessary? Hardly. Fun? Yes. It is the truth, but not the whole truth; and Kian opts to give her some slack, and instead answers: "You would be surprised, Healer Ingram. You would be surprised."

There are, no doubt, alternatives, but it's eminently useful. It opens all kinds of doors; and when it doesn't, the surprise and disconcert is nearly always hilarious to watch. He hasn't yet been in a situation where being able, and willing, to flirt with either sex has been a detriment as far as he's concerned.

Like now. Ingram's face is equal measures scandal, exasperation and, to a less extent but still delightfully present, intrigue. "I see." She doesn't quite sound like she sees at all, but doesn't appear to be about to say more; and after a short moment of silence while Kian watches with amusement, she nods and turns toward the bathroom. "I shall see you later this evening, then."

Kian bows. "Anon, then, Healer Ingram."

"Wait." Ingram turns suddenly, eyes narrowed. "The akh —"

"I shall take a taxi, Healer Ingram. It's not precisely a public place, but he wouldn't risk a non-magical witness, nor another murder." He smiles at her brightly. "How kind of you to be concerned."

"I am merely being logical," she says stiffly, and waves a hand as she turns as if to dismiss him. Laughing softly, Kian departs, and the Chamberlain's proximity to the city centre means he doesn't have to wait for a taxi. When he arrives he's slightly early, enough to get a table near a wall where he can at least see anyone approaching in the mirror. He does not take the chair near the wall, of course: if people believe he is unprepared, such small traps only benefit him.

His date arrives shortly after, and Kian rises to bow as she does, seeing her to her seat and making cheerful conversation. She has put in more effort than he, judging by her dress; but then, it's rather easier for men to have a suit prepared. She's unexpectedly easy to talk to over the menu, as well: not averse to making a quip about her work, if only to sidelong him to see how he responds. Someone, Kian decides, who likes to cut a date off early if one is unable to handle the realities of her job. He might be offended at her forgetfulness as to his knowledge, if it hadn't been a few days ago and the propensity of people to talk themselves out of something.

They're into the main before Kian is able to bring the conversation around to potential lightning-aligned metallurgists who might have crossed her, or someone else's, table. In the end she almost brings it up herself, by asking after the conclusion of the situation with Gregory; and that provides a convenient lead-in for Kian to show her the picture of the man from the car and gently question her about other corpses, under the guise of an extended 'investigation'.

Yes, she does recognise him; indeed, that is the man who had picked up the corpse, if she's not mistaken. No corpses in engineering have passed her table, though she *could* ask around, in exchange for the rest of the story there.

Kian will need to make up a suitable story, but he leaves an implication of urgency in his acceptance. Now they've seen

Carruthers face-to-face, he can't imagine that events will draw on for much longer. There is ... an impending sense of drawing to a close, provided they can first rescue the canopic jars belonging to the akh. If they can't, well, the information will be more useful. Still ...

Still. If this is someone capable of transferring their consciousness, as Geddo had implied, then Kian would dearly like to know: Just what does that list of mages have to do with it? Carruthers had only kept Gregory's corpse — and *only* Gregory's corpse. There is a dissonance here that he cannot quite distinguish.

The main course is done when Kian's phone rings, and with a glance at it and a smile at his date he excuses himself only briefly with a sincere apology. It isn't Ingram: it's the archivist at the church, which is rather less dire and quite important. Given how the church generally feels about him, particularly after the last time he dropped by, he had best not reject favours; not when he can't rely on their good will. Particularly since he hasn't told them about contacting the Egyptian church, and is likely to wind up solving something in their territory which they had not even known was happening.

It's a subtle pettiness, but it is one. Provided they discover it.

And then, of course, there's the fact of the skeleton and the soul-reaver. No; this is not a call he wishes to decline under the circumstances.

Kian finds a place near the bathrooms to take the call, answering with cheerful courtesy. "Ah, Archivist Albinson. I'm delighted to hear from you."

"Stuff that," she says, irritable. "Do you have to keep sending bobbies to our door? Everyone's bitching about you, you know."

"Merely performing my civic duty, Archivist," Kian answers blithely. "I'm surprised you called; I had expected an email. Is there some particular, and urgent, information you had to give?"

"Mostly wondering how you managed to get hold of a soul-reaver without knowing anything else about it."

"It wasn't difficult. I simply stumbled on the wrong, or the right, person at an opportune time, after all. Amazingly enough, that hardly requires knowledge; though I would, of course, be delighted to have my ignorance assuaged."

"At least you're good for that," she acknowledges, soothed by his willingness for learning. "It's a surprise, though. I'd have thought an Irishman would know by rote."

"Then I would be doubly delighted to have my ignorance assuaged," Kian answers, keeping the impatience out of his tone with some degree of effort. He has never, really, had the patience for people who draw out their point, even if it isn't something deliberate. "Pray, tell, Archivist. What are soul-reavers?"

"Well, that's the thing," she says, "we don't strictly know. But they came from Ireland. As far as historical records go, that much is clear. Only every bloody mage in Ireland over the course of their history has done everything they can to stop anyone outside it from finding out the details."

That is ... curious. Curious in a way that sets Kian's mind buzzing, while he feels detached. "And long enough ago that the younger haven't even heard of it," he murmurs. That's interesting, and more than mildly alarming. "I ought to be grateful, Archivist. Only your inimitable attention to history has allowed you to be aware of this."

What could possibly be so terrible that all the Irish mages throughout history have *erased* its origin from anyone outside the nation, and even those from within? Whatever it is, it's significantly older than four centuries. Such knowledge had stopped being commonplace by the time he was born.

Something tickles the back of his head, threads of a tune come together as yet unidentified, but only *barely* out of reach.

They came from Ireland. What, from Ireland, could possibly touch the soul? Be a weapon? Have so many copies — no, so many *pieces*.

The thought is there, alarming with its weight and yet still held in abeyance, and Kian is only absently listening to the archivist; and his gaze is equally absent out into the greater area of the restaurant. And then he sees, at his table, sitting with his date, is Carruthers.

"I beg your pardon, Archivist," Kian says, "but I must go. Thank you, very much, for your time." He ends the call before she can respond, his gaze still on the table, and as if just being watched draws his eye Carruthers looks up with a charming smile and their gazes lock, and there is an edge of predatory knowing in his eyes.

It would, Kian considers, be wise to walk away right this minute. There would be a back way. There's always a back way. It's unlikely that Carruthers would do anything to Kian's date; an innocent and without magic, her death would only draw attention Carruthers would not want. In fact Kian shifts, half-turning, quite intending to simply *leave*, when Carruthers's lips move and though Kian can't possibly hear his words over the restaurant's hubbub, they resonate loud and clear against his soul, like fingernails against a chalkboard.

"Why, Kian, aren't you going to join us?"

Carruthers beckons and Kian moves toward them entirely without intention, entirely without consent, and he reflects with detach that he owes Ingram an apology. Surely he is impaled on his own hubris; for though he *hadn't* yet met someone capable of manipulating names, it only means he was due.

He reaches the table and Carruthers's smile is graciousness velveting steel, and when Kian looks down at his date he sees her smile and eyes are dazed. She's already halfway through rising with her handbag on her shoulder, and out of habit — *purely* out of habit — Kian picks her coat off the back of her chair to help her into it.

"Thank you," she says, and adds dazed in a way which is surely an implanted suggestion, "I had a lovely time."

Kian bows. "If I have a need for professional discussion, I shall know to whom to come. I do apologise for shortening our dinner." He can at least be gracious about *this*, without needing coercion; and she brushes past, wandering off and likely home. Kian *hopes* home. "I suppose it would be too obvious if anything should happen to her on the street."

"Quite," says Carruthers in a tone of polite disbelief with an edge of disdain, as if he's been insulted by the mere airing of a possibility

that he would be less subtle than he is. "Do sit with me, Kian."
Kian sits. He doesn't have much of a choice. Carruthers gazes over
the table at him for quite a while, something dark in his eyes which
Kian does not particularly want to identify. "Where is the last of
my ... collection?"

Oh, dear.

For a moment Kian wrestles with the words in his mouth,
tripping off his tongue. "I gave it to somebody quite unwilling to
return it."

It ... isn't a lie, strictly. It isn't a lie at *all*, is the surprise; Kian
rather feels that it would grate more on his tongue if he'd tried it.
'Somebody', as opposed to 'something': and how interesting that
is, that he can tell the nuance in that wording without consciously
having divined the reason behind the difference. Where does lay
the line between conscious and subconscious truth-telling, when
commanded by one's name?

"I see," murmurs Carruthers, and he doesn't appear to think
Kian might be obfuscating, aside from the fact that he'd given no
names. Which, naturally, is immediately the next question. "Their
name, please, Kian."

"I don't know their name."

This *does* grate: it grates for though Kian has *suspicions*,
suspicions do not make a fact; and he does-not-know just enough
that it can be twisted, with how reluctantly he speaks to begin with.
This is ... highly uncomfortable.

"How reckless of you." There is most definitely displeasure
there. Kian smiles sunnily in response to it, and shrugs. The

name-bindings don't prevent him that. There's a phone ringing and it takes some time for Kian to realise it's in his pocket; and Carruthers's gaze flickers to Kian's coat, but they both sit in silence until it rings out. "I will allow you one question, Kian."

"How magnanimous," Kian murmurs. Questions, questions; hm. He can think of several, but there is only one, at this stage, to which he wants or needs any confirmation. "Why did you burn down the healer's clinic?"

He's watching. Surprise and then that disdainful affront cross Carruthers's face. "A healer's clinic? Why in the world would I burn down one of those? I'm not *insane*."

That remains to be seen, Kian thinks privately, but this is when a waiter comes with the bill, and Carruthers pays right there at the table; how kind of him. Then Carruthers rises and Kian follows without even a command, though not entirely with his consent.

"I suppose I'm going with you?" he says with dry asperity as he pulls on his overcoat, and Carruthers laughs, and doesn't even look over as he moves toward the exit, pulling on his coat.

"Quite, Kian. Quite."

Kian follows without fighting the demand, fishing in his pocket for his phone. 'Missed call from Healer Ingram' flashes on the screen, and he stows it as they exit; and without looking over Carruthers holds out his hand. This, Kian fights: and it feels like he's dragging raw muscle over glass, and does nothing in the end. He puts his phone in Carruthers's hand, and watches with a sense of dull resignation as it's tossed onto the road, and crushed under passing wheels.

He can only hope that phone call had been Ingram calling him with a location Verna had given her.

TWENTY-TWO
WALK SOFTLY

Once Kian's gone, and once Rosemary has had time to wrap her head around the idea of him being a cheerful, equal-opportunity seducer at the drop of a hat, it honestly is a nice evening in. For a given value of the idea which includes her clinic still being gone. She passes her time at first by doing her own regular health maintenance, since she's been neglecting for a few days now, and it really wouldn't do to be surprised by a menstrual cycle *now* of all times. When physical things are in order Rosemary settles down with the spare notepad, drawing out their facts on individual sheets and rearranging them on the table in hopes she'll see something this way that she hasn't when they were only ideas in her head.

The skeleton does not comment on any of this. It sits in the chair it seems to have claimed for its own, and it holds the knife, and its empty eye sockets stay fixed on her — at least, if it ever looks away, Rosemary certainly can't tell it's done so.

As an experience, this is both unsettling and reassuring.

She has a mess of impromptu mind-mapping on the table when Kian's tablet, carefully propped in view, lights up with a call. Good news, she hopes. Rosemary steps around the table to answer it.

It's a voice call by default — there are video options, she sees by the icons, but neither she nor the contact — Verna — has turned them on. "Hey, Kian," says the woman on the other end. Her voice is hard to pin down in terms of quality: she might be fifteen or fifty, Welsh or Ghanian, and Rosemary doesn't know how she'd begin to guess when she can't even name the accent. Or even if Verna *has* an accent in the first place. "Verna. I don't have everything yet, but —"

"Ah," Rosemary says, before anything can go too far. "A moment. This is Healer Ingram. I've been working with Kian; I'm not sure if he mentioned. He's out right now, but asked me to answer if you had urgent information."

"Oh," Verna says. Pauses. "Yeah, he's mentioned you, Healer. Sorry about your clinic. Finding the bastard's on my to-do list."

Rosemary winces. She appreciates the sentiment, but would just as soon not be reminded. "Thank you. First things first. What have you found?"

"Not much more on the metallurgist fuckery," Verna says, matter-of-fact, "but I turned up more on your asshole Carruthers. Interesting part, thirty-five years ago he disappeared for a week. He'd put in for leave from work, right, but only for two days. There was a police manhunt and everything. They finally got an anonymous tip, found him out in the boonies in some shitty abandoned apartment building. His kidnapper'd had a spontaneous heart attack, so hadn't gotten around to murdering the fuck out of him yet."

"... That's suspicious," Rosemary says, though that much is terribly obvious. A man who has ancient spirits at his call shouldn't be kidnapped at the drop of a hat. And, of course, she's well aware 'spontaneous heart attack' is sometimes what gets written on autopsy reports when the coroner simply can't find anything else.

Certainly, she herself could induce one, or a phenomenon that looks very much like it — but she wouldn't, save in the direst of circumstances.

"Abso-fucking-lutely," Verna says. "After that he just settled down. Nothing weird at all. *Most* people have something weird more than once in their fucking lives. Anyway, he's pretty sneaky, but I caught up to his records, fucking finally. He's got a place about an hour outside London. I got a satellite view of it, it's all sprawl and no taste." Rosemary *thinks* there's scorn in her voice, but she can't be quite sure. "I'm going to send over a bunch of data on that. I'll keep looking to cover all our bases, but this feels like it's the place he was trying most to hide. Shell companies and *goddamn* tax havens, you know?"

Rosemary does not, in fact, know, but she makes an agreeing sound like she does. "Is there anything else we should know?"

Verna hums a thinking sound, up and down and slightly discordant. "Don't think so," she says. "Not right now. I'll let you know."

"It's appreciated," Rosemary says. "I'll let Kian know you called." They'll want to follow this up quickly. She's not completely sure about tonight — travelling when there's lower visibility is perhaps sub-prime if they don't want to be ambushed by the akh again, and people are more likely to be home at night — but tomorrow morning, she suspects, will be the latest.

"Break a leg," Verna says, and the call closes, leaving only dead air.

Rosemary regards the tablet screen for a few moments. True to Verna's word, several notifications pop up before long. A shared contact card, colourfully named, featuring all of Carruthers's contact information, some image files which display the satellite photography Verna had been talking about. One of these has a rude image scribbled in it. There's also a latitude and longitude which open the maps application when Rosemary taps on the text. She plots a route via public transit — from here, it'd take about an hour and a half, accounting for the time to walk to various stations.

How terribly mundane, that their mysterious and dangerous foe can be bearded in his den for the mild inconvenience of train fare and shared seating.

The time's getting on past eight. Kian had expected to be back in the hotel by eight-thirty, with travel time taken into account, and there aren't any messages from him on Rosemary's own phone to advise of a delay. It would be reasonable, logically, to call him. She supposes Verna's information isn't precisely *dire*, but between the two factors, she rather thinks it's appropriate.

Besides, she'd like to know what Kian thinks of that peculiar kidnapping.

She calls, and he doesn't answer. The phone rings, and rings, and finally goes to voicemail.

"Well," Rosemary reasons aloud, phone still in hand, "he might have only gotten held up a little with good-nights."

The skeleton doesn't offer any answer. Not that she expected any, really. She regards the light in its eye sockets and doesn't find anything like an opinion in the depths of its skull.

Lovely.

Rosemary gives Kian another five minutes, and tries again. This time the phone goes straight to voicemail.

"Either he's turned it off, or run out of battery, or he's actively declining my calls." Rosemary taps the phone to her lips thoughtfully, paces the length of the room and back again. The skeleton's head swivels fractionally to track her position. It's much less unsettling than it used to be. "Or, I suppose, something might have happened to his phone."

8:15. She sets her phone down on top of her pages of connections and stands back from it. "Perhaps I'm being overly anxious. He's a man well grown, after all. Capable of taking care of himself, as we've seen."

The skeleton — what had Kian called it? Connor? It's as good a name as any — declines to comment.

Rosemary paces some more, as she's prone to; some kind of motion has always helped her think. Back and forth, and back and forth, and the very faintest rasp of bone along bone along shadow to keep her company. Kian *can* take care of himself, yes. He studies one of the immortal disciplines, whose students are more likely to die of murder than age, and he has made it this far. But, counter point: He also introduced himself to her by turning up in her clinic with a fence-post dangerously close to his femoral artery. He had walked right into a trapped room, and only luck had brought him out again intact. So: Competent, but fallible.

Third point: He has acted according to the social compact that more or less contains mages. He has not lied to her; he has offered her no harm; he has kept his word, when he's given it. A few days isn't much room to provide evidence counter to such things, she supposes, but until she's proven wrong, she offers him that trust. Which means: If Kian is not back by 8:30, and hasn't provided word to the contrary, then something is wrong, despite his assurance that being out in public would protect him.

He'd given his name to the man, without even a thought in his head for consequence.

Rosemary knows, in theory, that the magic of names is much, much less common out in the world, out from the lands where she was born. But she was taught her lessons well, and early, and grew up around those who could bend a thing to their will just by calling its name. The name she uses now, well-accustomed to it though she is, isn't the one she was born with — but it might work to control her anyway, what with how many legal documents it's on, and how much more *Rosemary* she is now than she was.

She doesn't care to find out. Hence, Heather Chandler.

And the akh ...

Something Geddo had said tickles at the back of her mind. That the mage who controls them must hold their names. If that isn't explicitly name-magic, it is certainly next door to it.

It's not quite 8:30 yet. Rosemary spends the next few minutes on a quick skimming of Wikipedia, gathering at least a vague idea of where the name sits in regards to ancient Egyptian beliefs. It's not enough to open more than a couple of additional sources, but she can at least make note of the presence of the name as vital to the existence of the soul. It's more than she had.

8:30 ticks by without any sign of Kian, and dread begins to curdle in her stomach. She looks for the address of the restaurant where he left it — maps it — finds the phone number without much additional effort. "Hello," she says, "I was wondering if you could tell me if a friend of mine is still there? I'm concerned his phone may have died."

She knows it sounds a bit flimsy, and isn't entirely surprised when the waiter who answered the phone is hesitant to answer. It's good staff practice, really, only she can't bring herself to appreciate it at the moment with Kian possibly in some trouble. "Look," she says, trying again. "He was on a date, I just want to make sure he gets home safely, and I'm not getting any answer from him. He's tall, dark-haired, dressed up — can you at least say, *if* he left, did he leave with someone or alone?" That, if she can get that answer, would be enough to confirm something.

There's a brief, thoughtful silence. "I think he left with his date, ma'am."

Hm. Well, the lack of word will be something to take up with him later, but at least it means he's not in serious danger. "I won't worry, then," Rosemary says. "I'm sure she'll take care of him."

"Huh?" The waiter sounds rather unexpectedly confused. "No, he left with a man. Maybe I'm thinking of a different person."

Relief vanishes like a glass of cold water down the back of her neck. "Older?" Rosemary inquires carefully. "Silver-haired, quite handsome?"

"Yeah, that's the one. Kind of a silver fox, right? You know him?"

"I do," Rosemary says distantly. Someone would have called the police if it didn't look like Kian left under his own will. "Thank you, you've been very helpful. I'm ... glad to know he's safe."

"Have a good night, ma'am."

Rosemary ends the call, and stares at the Connor-skeleton. "I *am* going to tell him that I was right to be cautious," she says, firmly, lining up a vision of the future that doesn't end with either her or Kian dead. Right. If Kian and Carruthers had left recently — damn. She hadn't asked when. It might have been any time after the start of the date.

In other words, she needs to leave now. "Come on," she tells Connor. "We need to go find Kian."

It stands up, and with one hand fumbles at its hood, apparently anticipating. Good she left it clothed — that's a delay she wouldn't like right now. A moment of some debate, and Rosemary takes Kian's tablet in addition to her own phone, thinking either there might be information or contact details stored there which might be helpful. He has a nice carrying-bag for it, easy to sling over the shoulder and shove other things into at need.

The stairs are quicker than the elevator, even with Connor managing the steps less nimbly than a living person would.

Outside Rosemary has to make a choice: The office, or the address Verna provided? The office is the known quantity, and Kian wasn't completely able to confirm if Carruthers had actually cleared out the adjacent room. The wards had seemed nasty enough that it could be a reasonable place to stash Kian — for a while, or until he met some worse fate. The office is also closer. But — assume Carruthers has some control of Kian, by name or some other method — then he won't worry about Kian getting free on his own. And a house outside London will be quieter. More isolated, if the photographs are anything to go by.

The helpfully morbid portion of her mind fills in that there will be no one to hear the screams. Rosemary rolls her eyes at herself. More than likely, there won't be any screaming, not if Kian's controlled.

The house, then. Rosemary maps out the address again — notes the time of the next train — quickens her pace.

She fumbles through the little mundanities of station and tickets, but despite a dropped card she and Connor make it onto the train before it leaves. Connor sits when Rosemary does, without having to be prompted, and her hip doesn't quite nudge it. Lingering scents, formalin and something a little meatier under that, catch Rosemary's attention. And there's something else, too, something very distantly reminiscent of the salt of the sea, but it's gone almost as soon as she places it. After a cursory inhalation or two to convince herself she's imagined the addition, she puts the distraction away and looks to Kian's tablet again as the train jolts into motion.

His contacts, she finds, are either helpfully labelled or not at all. There's Verna, for instance, but there's a few different options for her. A few church numbers, sorted by country. Various clerics, all of whom have Irish-looking names which won't be helpful on the drop of a hat. And — well, what does Rosemary expect from them? She's already moving, she's going to be the fastest response in any case. No one will be able to get any tools to her. She's competent enough, and she has a skeleton with a soul-reaver for a final solution if she *really* must, though it's certainly not a first resort.

In the end all Rosemary does is send a message to the most recent version of Verna's contact, the one she'd called from, letting her know of the situation and her own planned course of action. Verna responds rapidly, which is heartening, with a quick *Thx* and *i'll keep an eye on you*.

Rosemary thinks that's reassuring.

The intervening time stretches out long and painful. Rosemary hotspots the tablet off her phone and goes back to research.

She has cartouches and soul-parts, anecdotes about names chiselled off statues, rattling around the inside of her head by the time they get to the appropriate stop. It's a hasty research, and she's sure to lose half of it if she doesn't study properly, but that's fine. She doesn't need it long.

Off the train, Connor still at her heels, the mapped route directs them to a local bus-stop. That's all well and good, but the map application hasn't taken into account that there aren't any more buses at this hour. Rosemary takes the distance at a fast walk instead, and restrains the urge to cheat by upping her oxygen absorption. That takes a toll. She'll save it for if she really needs it.

The house looks a little more modest in person than it did from the remote satellite viewpoint, but there's still a sturdy wrought fence, and a middling span of grass between the road and the house. The gate is, inconveniently, locked. Rosemary supposes it's for the best Carruthers isn't anticipating company, but it's going to take additional time when she's painfully aware of every moment spent.

So she paces the fence-line, around to the back where the fence becomes brick instead of iron. It's more wooded here, mercifully, and some few of the trees have grown close enough that a reach should be possible. Rosemary hasn't climbed a tree in years; at least she has a climbing partner. The skeleton doesn't weigh much itself, but it doesn't have muscles to worry about straining, either, and between her direction and its supernatural abilities, they make it over more or less neatly.

Rosemary will feel it later. On the ground she assesses options and entrances. There will be wards, naturally, and she has precious little experience with them. If there was some alarm-ward on the fence, she's certainly already triggered it. They'd best move quickly. "Strip," she tells Connor, considering that the ever-chancy element of surprise isn't worth hampering whatever agility it may have.

The skeleton strips. It walks more soundlessly, now, and the reaver still clenched in its hand reminds Rosemary of something further. "He used his blood, didn't he," she says. "Can you follow that?"

It tilts its head at her, like nothing so much as a curious dog, and then it moves, barely denting the grass as it goes. After a few steps it pauses, looks back for her. Directives, overlapping.

"Very well," Rosemary says. She tucks her chin, flexes her hands, and wishes for nothing so much as a large stick.

Wishes will get her nowhere. Rosemary follows her skeleton, and hopes Kian's alive to wait for them.

TWENTY-THREE

SONG OF A WARHOUND

He never really falls unconscious, but the previous increments of time stretch backward like a blurry horizon. He can't quite find details: For starters, his name. He's vaguely aware of the sensation of his energy being drawn off, like he's being siphoned, but when he thinks on what 'siphoned' means, he only has vague memories about a sterile place and blood, and losing it. He can look around, at least, and there's nothing attached to him for siphoning; but he can't see over his head, and there lays an odd buzz.

He can't call out. The man who'd put him here had a specialised gag. It seems a bit superfluous, since he recalls the house being rather apart from most things, but that buzz overhead and the beat of his heart segue together in a way which seems, at times, oddly melodious. And he feels itchy to move.

219

It's cold on the stone table and his hands are bound to it, as are his ankles, and even through the haze he realises this is not at all a good thing. At least he isn't cold.

Still restless, though. All unknowing, his fingers tap out a tune on the stone, something which seems idle but isn't, like a looming monstrosity waiting where his knowledge of himself is hidden. It feels dangerous, but not lethal — at least not lethal to *him* — and he's curious enough to let his fingers have their say where his tongue cannot, even when it moves of its own volition against the gag like words are bound.

His heart beats the drum, all steady bass against the tune ringing in him.

The door cracks open and something scuttles down the stairs, something which rattles ever so faintly in a way which, coincidentally or not, seems like counterpoint to the tune against stone. Someone else follows, footsteps a louder thud, and not nearly as melodious.

"Kian?"

The voice is hushed and a little shocked. He turns his head and lifts his eyes, such as he can with the rattle and the footfalls above him; but within moments the woman who spoke is within his sight, frowning and face half in darkness owing to the shadow cast by her luminescent hair, and pressing a hand to his forehead. He blinks wordlessly and then, quite abruptly, shivers violently at the sudden chill down his spine.

His fingers have still not stopped playing the song in them.

"Just a moment."

She vanishes save a wisp of her sleeve, and there's a pause; and then she grunts and something strikes stone, and something else shatters.

Memories come back in a flood and so does energy, and Kian's limbs twitch with something not quite adrenaline, not quite magic, but a combination of the two which disrupts the tune he had going. Ingram is back in a moment, peering into his face, and Kian nods; and within another moment she has the gag unbuckled and tugged off, and thrown aside in a fit of justifiable malice.

Kian coughs before he can speak, his mouth dry, as Ingram works loose the bonds on his wrists and ankles. *Now* he's shivering in the cold, and by unhappy corollary that makes him realise he's nude as the day he was born, which is just lovely.

"Water," Kian says, and coughs again. Ingram glances around as he stretches out his limbs; there's a glass of water on the smaller table above his head that she fetches, set aside with a myriad of tools which look like they belong in a museum's display, and Kian drains the glass before trying to get on his feet.

"If we hurry, we might be able to get out before he realises I've found you," she says in a fit of adrenalised optimism, and naturally this is when the door opens and Carruthers's voice rings out, fluid in a language Kian does not know. From the side and the long alcove behind the stairs there's a puff of shadow and a long discordant harp-note; and the akh form in swirls of dust and bone, long snouts gleaming and ears flicking. There are many of them, more than Kian remembers from the street; and though most are jackals some are not, and isn't that interesting? He'd wondered what Carruthers had done with his previous victims' souls. Probably what he meant to do with Kian's, also.

The skeleton turns toward the akh, lifting the reaver threateningly; it gives them pause — just enough. Kian snatches up the blood-letting knife, the one that is not glass, with words on his tongue but not his lips as he brings it down to cut long across the meatiest part of his thigh, an impending scar to join the others there. He keeps the knife against flesh just long enough for blood to gather on the edge, then lifts and flings it at the skeleton; and *now* he sings, something vicious and triumphant. The skeleton's jerk is surprise, and then it straightens; and the way it stands is proud and fierce, and not at all skeletal; and green light burns in its sockets, lending something like an eerie wreath around its skull.

"— Nocon fetar cóich in cú Culaind asa Murthemniu, acht ra fetar-sa tra imne bid forderg in sluag sa de —"

"Are you insane?!" Carruthers screams, and Kian grins at him in a way more a baring of teeth, and drops the knife, and stamps his foot for drumbeat, claps his hands for the crotchets; and if Carruthers says anything else at all, even to use Kian's name, it's lost in the pound of heartbeat and music in his soul which had only been waiting for opportunity.

Piercing calls strike up from the akh, as if in response to Carruthers' sudden fear, and the skeleton beckons at the shadows. One of the akh lunges and is caught by the shadow-dust body of a hound almost the height of a man's shoulder, and in seconds the akh dissolves under powerful jaws. The rest keen and circle, backing away; and there's another hound nearby, circling around

Kian and Ingram protectively from behind. Kian can hear them growling, and cannot be sure it's a sound he's hearing with his soul or his ears, or whether Ingram can hear it at all.

A shaft. I need a shaft! The skeleton beckons impatiently, and *this* is a voice that only Kian can hear, imperious and demanding, in a language of his nation so old that he shouldn't understand it: And yet.

"— A gae bulgae mar-domber cenmothá a chlaideb sa sleg, fer i furchrus bruitt deirg dobeir a choiss for cach leirg —"

With hands drawn apart in one smooth motion Kian weaves a spear-shaft out of shadow and tosses it to the skeleton; and though it should, strictly speaking, dissolve under anyone else's touch, it slaps into the skeleton's bony palm like timber into flesh. The shadows swell over the hilt of the dagger the skeleton presses to the end, forming around it and settling as though forged to it; and when he straightens it's to throw.

The spear impales Carruthers through the chest, hard enough to make him stagger even standing at the foot of the stairs; and then he laughs, breathless owing to the weapon in his torso. His lips move but Kian can't hear the words; and he stops quite abruptly in any case when barbs of shadow burst from every orifice, narrower than the shaft as a whole and each speeding unerringly toward the canopic jars where Carruthers' organs are kept, lining the shelves over the tombs of the akh.

Only one is tipped with the shard of the Gáe Bulg: and that one strikes Carruthers' heart in a tinkle of breaking clay. Shadows dissolve all around Carruthers' body and he collapses at the top

223

of the stairs; but the akh remain, stirring and whispering restlessly beyond the circling hounds. Kian closes his mouth on the end of The Foretelling and for a moment there's a discordant note of song trying to continue which feels like he's been punched internally; but his mouth is firmly closed and after a moment the song lapses, complete *enough*, but without closure. The way the skeleton turns to him seems once more like surprise; and then it salutes with its dominant hand, cheerful despite being made only of bone.

"What —" Ingram begins, sounding shaken, and then Kian sags with the deluge of exhaustion and instead she grips his arm to hold him up with the help of the stone altar.

Kian coughs, and points past the akh. "The tombs."

"You're bleeding." She reaches for the table at the head of the altar, where the glass of water had been accompanied by a basin and a hand-towel; Carruthers had certainly been prepared. Kian takes it from her to press it against his thigh himself with a grimace of a groan. She sighs in exasperation. "Let me —" He feels the chill which is her reaching magically for the injury from his shoulder, running disconcertingly down his spine, and before he can warn her off she reels back with a shudder without releasing his arm. "... I'll give it a bit."

Kian grins, the kind of fierce grin owed after a battle, all victory and readiness to cut. He restrains himself from that. Mostly. "Quite. Healers never seem to like blood-letting wounds made for the sake of raising someone. The tombs — I'll be alright leaning."

... Or possibly sitting, because the throb in his leg is starting to set in and his knees feel awfully weak. He lowers himself, very carefully, to the floor; and that's also stone, and just as cold, and at least *clean*. Nevertheless, he rests his head back, and tries not to shiver. "I don't suppose my clothes are down here."

"I can't see them at a glance," says Ingram, very nearly archly, "but it's hard to tell when we're surrounded in such a way. Where is the — soul-reaver?"

The catch in her voice says she recognised what it was just as surely, and Kian wonders — just what *do* the elfs of England think of Cú Chulainn? That's going to be interesting, given that technically the skeleton belongs to Ingram. "I think it fell against the wall. I doubt the akh will be able to pick it up now."

Not now he's gone ahead and spoken its name, and to whom it belongs. The skeleton still watches the akh, standing in the manner of readiness while its wolves circle; even in his own head, Kian does not quite dare to speak the name, as he hadn't quite had to sing it.

Ingram nods shortly after a moment, her gaze on the skeleton; and after another moment she beckons. "I need something to escort me to the tombs."

The skeleton turns and gives her a long look, the light in its sockets not at all dimmed; and then its finger-bones card through shadowed fur, and it points. One of the hounds turns to snap at the akh nearest Ingram, and the akh scatter with discordant rustles; and, step by step, Ingram is guarded to the tombs.

Kian, for his part, chooses to close his eyes; and then the muffling warmth of darkness attempts to suck him under, so he opens them and glances toward the skeleton, watching the eerie green light against the walls. "And do talk to me about what you're doing,

Healer Ingram," he adds, a little drowsily, "since I rather doubt falling asleep, at this juncture, is a terribly wise idea."

"Please don't," answers Ingram, and adds dryly: "It would be difficult to have to carry you out over my shoulder, and no doubt undignified given your state of undress."

On the bright side, Kian is still capable of laughing.

TWENTY-FOUR

TERMINAL VELOCITY

L amentably, removing the metaphorical head of the serpent doesn't solve the issue of the akh, still swirling angry almost-solid threats, kept at bay by shadow-hounds which also shouldn't exist. The one piece of fortune they do have is that Carruthers has kept their relics here: Their tombs, what remains of their physical forms, and likely their names.

The basement is full of impossible legends.

One of the two shadow-hounds, in nearly the same apparent state of flux as the akh, pads by her side, snapping teeth at anything that drifts too close. Its posture is alert, fierce but not indiscriminately rabid. Rosemary very pointedly does not think about where it came from or why it is here; only that it *is* here, and for the moment, it is her guard-dog.

The far wall of tombs, if she means to call them that, is a modest affair. Where the rest of the basement is modern enough, solid cement or clean-polished wood, this wall is rough-hewn stone; it looks like it's been shaped by hand. There are several careful alcoves, like shelves or altars, and in each is a series of jars, carven with images and set in specific order. Each, too, has a name: but the name is carved into a small flat stone, and the characters surrounded by lines. Rosemary knows from her reading that a name could be protected by a cartouche, but this isn't the same as the examples she saw — the multiple layers of encircling makes her think of hiding something, or tucking it inside something else. A shield, and then something more. Carruthers had been doing something to Kian's name which Rosemary suspects darkly would have ended up in a similar state, if she had not interceded by vandalising the offending masonry — it had seemed only partially complete.

Not all of the names are Egyptian. Some of them have very recognisable script, contemporary sounds. Carruthers has picked apart souls both ancient and modern.

Rosemary has no idea what to do with them. She could certainly destroy what's there — there were stone-working tools by Kian's table, and she has frustration to loose — but it would not, she thinks, properly set these souls to rest. "An hour-long Wikipedia binge is not nearly enough to conduct proper funerary rites," she says over her shoulder, trying for dry and managing brittle. "I'm going to get into your call history and try contacting the Egyptian Temple. You may need to vouch for me."

"My call history?" Kian says, distantly, dizzily. Rosemary categorises symptoms of catastrophic blood loss, tries to counterbalance them against kidnapping and name-magic hangovers. The cold and lack of clothing can't be doing him any favours, but unless she starts stripping herself, there's little to be done right now. "— Ah. You have my tablet? Good thinking."

She'll file stripping toward the bottom of her list of possible solutions. "I needed to do something on the train," she says, shifting the bag across her body and rummaging through it. The house wireless is encrypted, but mobile signal in the basement isn't as bad as it could be, so she sets up the hotspot again, all the while conscious of the discordant shadows that would probably happily kill them in a moment. Despite that obstacle, her hands have actually stopped shaking, which is either a good sign or a terrible one. "Unfortunately, surface-level expertise hardly makes up for a lifetime of learning. Tell me you called the Cairo temple on video — no, of course not, it was on your phone." Which is wherever Kian's clothes are, which makes it useless. Rosemary tabs through recent messages anyway, trying to scan without prying.

"The contact lists are synced," he says helpfully. "Check the email?"

Fiddling with technology under these circumstances is not, precisely, her favourite occupation. Rosemary gets into his email, and without prompting finds the exchange where he provided images for reference to Geddo; and in a later response to that same email, a concrete phone number which a messaging service will accept.

Now she just has to hope someone in Cairo will actually answer, when it's already past midnight there, again.

The tablet rings, and rings. Rosemary taps the edges of it, sidelong eyes the hounds and then the skeleton again.

— No. Not the skeleton. She's pretending he doesn't exist, either, because she honestly cannot know that right now. There are only so many things with which she can cope at once. She turns her face away from him, and surveys the akh instead, the array of shadows set against shadows. When she looks closely she can pick out individuals, almost, and there are those that have dog-like — jackal — heads, and those that certainly do not. This, if she had to guess, also fits with the mix of ancient and modern names.

The call ends without being picked up. Rosemary redials, apologising mentally as she does, and focuses intently on every electronic ring. She is almost certainly going to be getting someone out of bed, at this rate.

"Healer Ingram?" Kian's voice, a little more pronounced about the accent.

She twitches when she hears him, as she would flinch for anyone who startled her out of thought. Ah. She'd stopped talking to him, and it's rather an inexcusable lapse at this point, when focus might make a difference. "No one's answering," she says. "As a last resort I can start breaking things, but there's no guarantee that wouldn't backfire. Better to have someone like Geddo tell us what to do, if possible."

"Ah," Kian says distantly. "Of course. Sound reasoning."

Rosemary hunkers down on the spot, tablet braced on her knees. Like this the shadow-hound is higher at the shoulder than her head is. It turns its nose briefly as if to sniff her, as if shadows and stories have working olfactory systems, and then resumes snapping at anything that comes too nearby. "It's taking a while," she says, wishing there were better news to report. She's starting to wonder if it's the time, as she initially thought, or instead the dodginess of a mobile hotspot in a basement. "It always seems like Egypt should be further ahead in time than it is."

"Such is the magic of the curvature of the globe." His dryness is rallying. Good.

"I suspect that's physics," Rosemary says, and redials.

This time success; this time within three rings the call connects. "Another emergency, Kian?" comes the now-familiar voice from the other end, and relief strikes like a hammer. "At this hour, one hopes."

Rosemary stands, keeping careful hold of the tablet. She doesn't blame Geddo for preferring they have good reason to wake him. "It's Healer Ingram," she says, turning up the volume as she does. "We've found the akh, and their — canopic jars? Their names? Everything that remains, so far as I can tell. However, they're rather upset, and cannot be kept at bay forever. I hoped you might have some advice."

'Rather upset' is an understatement. She's starting to sound like Kian.

"And the one who held them?" There's a note of warning she doesn't quite understand in Geddo's voice.

"Dead," Rosemary says. "Inescapably." A spear that branches, that penetrates through every vein —

She's not thinking about it.

"You sound very sure," Geddo says. "There are tricks. If he kept his heart outside his chest ..."

"I know." Rosemary eyes the akh. "Ask Kian, later, what he did." Summoned to him — no. *Woke up* what he'd already summoned, a story Rosemary knows best as *'This is why we don't do what your mother did, child'*. Of all the reckless things to do—! But Rosemary is still telling herself that this particular thing is not happening, and so she stops, and she puts it away, fingers white-knuckled on the edge of the tablet. "For now, please take my word for his death. The akh? I think I can send a video, although the quality may be poor."

There's a pause from the other end. "I will look forward to hearing that story," Geddo says, rather too peaceably for the situation in Rosemary's opinion. "Video will be useful, if you can send it."

Rosemary does a quick sweep of the screen for likely icons — notes that the hair on the back of her neck stands on end every time a shadow flows too close for her liking — enables video. For a moment there's an image of her mildly pixelated face, pale as ever and shaded grey with wear and poor lighting; then she flips the video to the back lens and does a slow pan around the room. She tries not to catch Kian in the video sweep, though a quick flash of pale skin and blood tells her she isn't entirely successful. Primarily, though, she shows the akh, and unavoidably the hounds with them, and then a careful angling across the wall of tombs and back again.

"Those dogs," Geddo says, beginning a question.

"The akh," Rosemary repeats. She cannot and will not explain the hounds.

"... Scan back over the top row again, please."

She appreciates the concession. "Kian," she says, her head turned over her shoulder toward him, "you will be the one explaining all of this later, just so you're aware."

At first there's not a reaction, which has her heart doing something unpleasantly jolting. Then a moment later Kian stirs again, says "*Mngh*," very firmly. "That hardly seems fair."

He's taking years off her life with stress, is what he's doing. Rosemary keeps back outright displeasure with the reminder that anything he is causing her, he's paying back in full with pain and danger as they speak. "It's going on your invoice," she says, with the sort of pleasantness that she hopes will tell him she will accept no argument on this note. "It's going to be a very long one."

"I'm sure it is, Healer Ingram." Still a little distant, but he sounds more alert now. Perhaps threatening him with the invoice is the way to go.

From the tablet, Geddo clears his throat, and automatically Rosemary looks down again, though there's nothing to see — he hasn't enabled video on his end, if whatever device he has even has the capability. "The proper rites would not be feasible right now," he says. "But I can remind them of the parts of them which are physical, and tell them to rest. If the man who held them is dead, they will listen, and I will have people in London to collect the remains as soon as a plane can have them there. Within the day."

"He's dead," Rosemary says for the third time, and turns up the volume on the tablet, as far as it will go. "Whatever you mean to do, please go ahead."

"Very well." And there is a pause, and then a language she doesn't know. It's a beautiful sound, she thinks, but she can't even tell where the words divide, so all there is really to do is to let the syllables wash over her and watch what happens as he speaks.

The akh perk up little by little — the jackal-headed ones first, all at once when Geddo hits a certain phrase, as though he has called their names. The others take longer to listen. One has come a little too near Kian, and Rosemary sees him shift, and the hound that had stayed with the skeleton now lopes in with teeth clashing. The akh falls back, its shadows caught in hound-jaws before it can harm Kian, slips away seeming lesser than it was and having done no damage. The guard-dogs do their job well; so have they ever done. Culann's hound knows his business —

Rosemary is not thinking about where the dogs came from.

The last, too-determined straggler finally looks toward Rosemary and the tablet with Geddo's voice, slinks toward them scattered, slip-stepping across the basement floor almost in pieces. Rosemary can't even tell what sort of creature's head this one bears, so twisted up and warped it is.

Geddo, she thinks, sounds compassionate.

Catching the attention of the akh has the side-effect that all of them are now pointed directly at Rosemary, and a tablet with a potentially dodgy connection is little shield; but it holds, and it holds, and Geddo keeps talking. Some of the akh start to eddy toward the wall, slow and reluctant, pooling together and apart again in strange, layered-shadow intersections. There's a rhythm in his voice, a rise and a fall Rosemary would almost call waves. She finds she nearly wants to rest, too, that she could very easily sit down against the far wall and simply sleep for a while, but —

There are too many things to do. Rosemary bites the inside of her cheek and reminds herself that she has a list of responsibilities at least three feet long.

As the akh move faster, some pass behind her, around her, moving now with more enthusiasm but too close for comfort, so close her hair stirs. The dog tasked to escort her thrums a warning she feels jarring her spine, rattling her teeth — less a sound than an idea of a sound, passing straight from intent to feeling without stopping in the open air between.

But no harm comes: that which passes is more interested in rest, now, than in the living.

Geddo keeps speaking for a long several seconds after the last of the akh spirals down toward the jars that hold the last earthly pieces of them. One rattles softly; there is a sound like a sigh.

All is still.

"Will that keep?" Rosemary wants to know, when she has stood there some few moments into the quiet. She turns to survey the rest of the room quickly.

Kian is still slumped against the table. Still very naked, not that she had expected that to change. The skeleton had been standing near him — it moves, now, to reclaim the fallen blade, picks it up and turns it over in hands too nimble to be made only of bone. The

235

hound which had defended Kian tracks after skeletal footsteps, diminishing with each one, finally settles between the skeleton's ankles as a tumbling shadow-puppy. It yawns to bare tiny dark fangs, and finally subsides into sleep and darkness. Rosemary's erstwhile protector, too, has laid down, curled around with its tail draped over its nose, and by the time her gaze lands on it, the hound has already lost distinction, becomes only an unusual darkness.

"It should," Geddo says, with a firmness Rosemary really does appreciate. "At least long enough for some of my priests to get to you. I would not, however, disturb the jars if you can avoid it."

"We can't stay here the entire time, either." Rosemary disables the video before she accidentally lets Geddo get a good look at the skeleton, and she goes to Kian, setting the tablet on the table as she crouches next to him. "Kian's injured, and it doesn't like me."

"It doesn't like your magic, Healer Ingram, let us be precise." Kian's eyes are slits, but he's certainly awake enough to be annoying. Rosemary sets a hand on his shoulder and tentatively reaches out again. It had been unpleasant last time, a fever-heat of sensation that reached *toward* her, and whether it wanted to consume or to wound she couldn't say. She had left off feeling like she'd been incautious about taking something out of the oven. "It won't have been long enough."

She certainly has to *try*. But no — she can already tell it will burn her. Reluctant, Rosemary pulls her awareness back, scowling. Kian's skin under her hands is cooler than is optimal, which is odd contrast to the heat that puts her off. Concerns for infection nag at the back of her mind. At least, though Carruthers' clothes won't be wearable, she may be able to use them for better bandaging. "When *will* it have been long enough," she demands.

Kian shrugs. "It varies," he says. "Really, who can say?"

"You're the one with more experience in this particular arena," Rosemary points out. She's really trying not to be acerbic with him, since he was recently kidnapped, but the injury is his own fault.

A gently staticky clearing of a throat tells her that Geddo is still on the line. "It has to matter," he says, not unkindly. "If Kian injured himself to raise or control something, then the pain, the willingness to risk, the bleeding — all these are as much part of the magic as the blood itself. You cannot simply take them away, Healer Ingram, as much as it may be in your nature to end pain. If the wound is healed as soon as it is made, where is the cost?"

Rosemary hates, very much, that he makes sense. But — wait. "I healed you when we first met, without issue," she says to Kian. "And you used that blood to keep Gregory moving, did you not?"

Kian flaps a hand at her, as though to wave that idea off. "Dead blood," he says. "You will note I had to constantly refresh the tie. A useful medium, but as a conduit of power, slightly short-lived. That was not a wound I gave myself, either."

The bleeding at least seems to have slowed a little, but Rosemary doesn't trust that. She straightens to go to Carruthers, intending to cannibalise what of his clothing she can. Better than nothing.

She's half expecting him to have turned to dust, or shrivelled up, or to find some ancient preserved mummy in the businessman's clothes. She does not. He's just a man, only now he's a dead one. And his shirt is almost uselessly blood-soaked about the chest, too.

The skeleton now standing motionless in the corner has its knife back. She cannot ask for its use. Instead Rosemary sorts through the stone-working tools left behind. The chisel isn't much, but she can snap threads with it, and between that and some determination she has the sleeves of the shirt off in short order. She pulls them off Carruthers's stiffening arms and returns to Kian, intending to put a little better pressure on the wound at the *very* least.

"Precisely how many disciplines do you use?" she asks as she works, intending that Kian should have to talk and keep his focus on her. "Blood, and song, and shadow, and death — where do they become the other?"

She doesn't get an answer. Kian opens his mouth as if to speak, and then there is shouting from up the stairs, and bright lights through the doorway. "Police!" someone calls. "Anyone down there?"

Judging by the sound of boots, they are not waiting for an answer. Rosemary grits her teeth and raises her voice. "Here! We're here!"

Spirits within and without, she hopes they don't notice the skeleton.

"Lovely," Kian says thinly, tilting his head back to rest against the stone behind him. "I have always wanted to be naked in front of a large group of people."

Rosemary doesn't know how seriously to take him; and then the police are there, and it is rather a moot point.

TWENTY-FIVE

FOR REMEMBRANCE

Kian spent overnight in the hospital. It might have been more, but the gash really wasn't all that bad once stitched; the main issue was the chill and the blood loss. Kian acceded to the night given he didn't want to develop pneumonia, which was an unfortunate risk in these circumstances owing to a necromancer's tendency to give up their warmth overly readily. The hard part about it all was when the nurses reported the other scars on his thigh, and the ones on his wrists; not as many as there could have been, of course, but in a pinch he does tend to cut more deeply than strictly necessary for a bit of blood, it's true.

Still, it meant he'd had to sit through a mandatory session with the resident psychologist just long enough for the hospital to satisfy itself that they weren't letting someone truly suicidal out on their own. Kian would have found it tiresome, if he didn't appreciate so much the attention to detail and to duty.

It means that when he comes out, dressed in a suit Ingram had delivered sometime that morning, he's surprised to find Geddo waiting for him in the lobby rather than Ingram herself.

It must be Geddo: there's no one else it could be. Shorter than Kian, and with brown skin leaning to the darker side, and the kind of air of patient inexorability. He could have been waiting there for hours, such is the air he gives off, but when Kian checks his pocketwatch it surely can't have been so long; not given the need to fly over. Somehow Kian had not quite been able to imagine him in clothes more common outside the temple, and yet. He looks like a youthful grandfather waiting.

Geddo rises when Kian comes toward him and bows, more deeply than he frankly did of his own high priest.

"Thank you," Geddo says benevolently, and though he doesn't smile there is something warm in his face, which becomes warmer after he's examined Kian for a moment. Kian has not missed the sensation of an older and far more experienced cleric seeing straight through him, but there it is. He can hardly claim Geddo has not been useful; particularly as a detached voice in the basement of Carruthers's house once the police arrived, telling them about the priceless Egyptian artefacts which had been stolen and which Kian had been attempting to recover on his behalf.

Kian lifts his eyebrow. "Seen everything to your content?"

"It's enough," Geddo agrees, and smiles then, slow and bidding, and turns toward the doors. "Walk with me."

"Wherever to?" Kian asks jovially, falling into step. He contemplates, for just a moment, not matching his pace; but he is still weary, and there's really no need to be pointed, except that Kian doesn't know how *not* to be where authority is concerned. There is authority and then there is authority.

"Wherever you are going," says Geddo implacably, with the result that they wind up walking a few streets in silence. Kian opts, in the end, to head for the Chamberlain: Walk, not taxi. They're close enough, and he doesn't feel this conversation would be well-had anywhere else. He also feels, unexpectedly, slightly vulnerable without the skeleton trailing along behind.

"Have you acquired your remains?" Kian asks, to put off the moment of explanation, and Geddo nods without looking over.

"The police, as we thought, had no desire to prompt international ill-will by resisting overly much. The canopic jars were secured from Carruthers's house as well as I could hope from heathens and have suffered no damage." He says heathens almost blithely — *almost* — in the manner of someone who came to English from the route of different languages first, until it's impossible to tell whether it's a joke or not. "Some of my temple are at the station to repack them now. We brought an archaeologist who will be able to support our right to claim with any other authorities."

"Good." It is good. Kian had not been looking forward to finding out how much of a kerfuffle that might have been; but, perhaps not unexpectedly, the Egyptian Temple is already well-versed in claiming what has been stolen.

"I wish to thank you," Geddo goes on as if Kian had not said anything between, nor even looking around. He walks with his hands clasped behind him, at an unmistakable stroll: Not an amble, nothing quite so lacking purpose, but without any urgency at all. "In truth, the tombs needed only to be destroyed to erase the threat the akh represented. Certainly it would have been the more logical action. Yet you did not resort to violence, and now we are able to return two-dozen lost souls home."

"I find logic does not always run in straight lines," Kian says dryly, thinking of the assassin he'd killed and then released to her sister.

"That," says Geddo, "is not a knowledge I have come to expect from anyone under seven centuries."

"Oh? You know many people over seven centuries, do you?"

Geddo does look at him then, and smiles, and does not answer; but it's the kind of smile which makes a shiver run down Kian's spine, and Kian looks away first. Geddo does not. He merely waits.

In the end Kian sighs. "I may have summoned a possible deity." He does not really expect a response, but he does wait a beat to see how Geddo reacts, out of the corner of his eye; and there is no reaction at all. Perhaps that's to be expected. As old as Geddo is said to be, gods were probably thick upon the ground back in the day. "Were you aware that soul-reavers originated from Ireland?"

"I was not," Geddo admits, and finally looks forward. "They've been in existence long before even my birth."

"They're the shards of the Gáe Bulg. The spear of Cú Chulainn."

243

Now there is silence, and if it is not precisely *shocked* silence, it's the contemplative sort which needs a few moments to collect. "I see," Geddo says eventually, and nods. "Yes, I begin to see."

He slants his gaze sideways much in the same way Kian has been watching him, and since they're both looking at each other anyway Kian stops and faces him, ignoring how they've forced the other pedestrians to move around; and Geddo does so as well. Kian isn't sure what he expects, precisely, but he's waiting for *something*. It's probably foolish to hope to win in patience. The high priest of the Egyptian Temple, they say, is over a thousand years old.

But he finds he doesn't have many words to say, either, because Geddo's look is more examining even than before, and unexpectedly it's Geddo who does break the silence, his tone oddly gentle. "Are you well, Kian ó Maolomhnaigh?"

"I don't feel as though I'm about to have something parasitic attach itself to my soul, if that's what you mean," Kian says, dry and a little repressive.

"That isn't what I asked."

Kian sighs and looks up over the overcast sky, as it so often is hereabouts, and considers. The truth is that he's been hearing songs whenever he sits quietly for a time, or when he's about to sleep or just waking; and he knows what song it is, naturally, but even still — a necromancer shouldn't be able to hear any song but their own in such circumstances. And yet.

"I don't know," he admits. "It isn't often someone summons a god, and I did so rather accidentally, before I realised what I'd done." There's a beat of expectant silence which passes for a question, and Kian explains, "I used the reaver to mark Healer Ingram's clinic skeleton. I thought its discipline would animate the skeleton long enough to guard us while we slept, or while I was absent. All the stories I've ever heard speak of reavers like vicious tools, not feeling shades — but then the skeleton refused to give it back, and quickly learned things it should not have without a brain." Like how to dress itself.

"Some reavers may still be like that," Geddo points out, and Kian inclines his head. Just because the original reavers came from the Gáe Bulg doesn't mean someone didn't manage to create replicas from scratch. It's inconsequential currently, except as the barest salve to his previous, flawed logic. Geddo turns to start walking again, and Kian falls silently into step; and this time it's Geddo who looks at the sky.

"You're not the first to have tried to claim a reaver in such a way, though the other instances of which I've heard resulted more lethally."

"I can imagine," Kian says dryly. "I supposed the same." He's an Irishman, after all; and Culann's hound is quintessentially Irish. He heard the call of a brother-in-arms, and obeyed, loyal as the hound he was in life. They round the corner and The Chamberlain stands down the street, and Geddo holds out a hand to stop them again, turning gravely toward Kian.

"I am curious," he says. "Songs such as that want for singing. I am impressed by your strength of will to cut it short; but more to the point, I wonder why you did so."

Kian looks at him with faint surprise, and then smiles. Over a millennia old does not mean omniscient, it seems. "Because of how it ends," he says. "Cú Chulainn was said to be under two geasa: One to never refuse food from a woman, and one to never eat dog meat. The Morrigan disguised themself as a woman on the road and offered him meat he could not eat. Regardless of his choice, he broke a geas, through no real fault of his own." Kian glances toward The Chamberlain, contemplating. Ingram is probably waiting there; he cannot imagine she's found a better place to stay since yesterday. "He was prophesised to have been born during the Ulster Cycle, to almost single-handedly win a war for his people, to be subject to restrictions he could not choose and suffer the fate of killing people he held dear regardless of his desire; and, worse, to lose his sense of self given enough rage. I summoned him practically by accident. It seemed ... a faithless, unconscionable act, to throw him away as soon as he was no longer convenient. And besides —" He stops, hums a note of a song still his, even if, these days, threaded with something else. "Ireland is a nation of war and tragedy. It seems to me that if its future should become otherwise, someone must stop the cycle somewhere."

He glances back to find Geddo looking quietly approving.

"You are quite impressive, Kian," he says, and Kian smiles back, less sunnily than he would have anyone else, but with more assurance.

"I'm quite aware, yes."

"Don't lose sight of why," Geddo warns, but it's a warm kind of warning. "Forgetting is the path of hubris." He turns toward the street to signal an empty taxi heading toward The Chamberlain in search of fares.

"Aren't you at all concerned that there's a godling of Ireland wandering about?" Kian asks, almost bemused. He certainly isn't going to tell the English Church, let alone the Irish one; he can only imagine the uproar it would cause. And that's among those of his own kind, who dream of summoning power to bend to their will. The rest of the mages? Kian shudders to think.

"Not anymore," Geddo answers without turning around as a taxi pulls up. "I dare say there are some who would think I ought to do something about it; but you have shown kindness to my people where others would not have. I've no inclination to exact a price out of fear. Indeed, I prefer to offer you sanctuary, were it ever necessary." He opens the door and looks up over it, his gaze even and inexorable in the fashion of someone who has not only lived quite a long time, but knows and understands what he has done with the time. "Do give the good healer my thanks, also."

"I will." Kian watches him get into the taxi and pull away, and stays there for a few minutes more, wondering. The way Geddo said that makes it seem almost like an expectation; and, after some moments contemplation, Kian can't deny that he ought to expect it also. He does have a habit of not endearing himself to people; the choices he's made tend to set him on a path where he alienates those who should be his allies.

He just hadn't been expecting someone to do the exact opposite. It's ... unique.

After some moments Kian shakes his head and continues to The Chamberlain, where the receptionist helpfully confirms that Ingram has remained in the room for which he's still paying. He's tired and his thigh is sore after walking the distance and so he takes the elevator, and when he opens the door the first thing he sees is — Connor is most likely the safest way of approaching things — the first thing he sees is Connor looking up from the armchair where he's seated, polishing the reaver with a hand-towel stolen from the bathroom. Connor salutes cheerfully with the blade, and goes back to polishing.

"Kian," says Ingram from her place at the desk, swivelled to see who enters. Her tone is arch, and Kian bows, cheerily sarcastic.

"Healer Ingram. I'm sure you're delighted to see me."

"Quite." Her mouth smooths explicitly so as not to twitch up. "I trust you're sufficiently healed?"

"Sufficiently," Kian agrees, coming into the room and hanging up his coat. "Some stitches, of course." It's for the best, given the kind of wound it is; her magic will never really enjoy touching that particular injury. "It seems the canopic jars are adequately attended, and Geddo asked me to deliver his thanks to you for opting for the more difficult and humane route with the akh. The police?"

"They're closing the case," Ingram says, with the sort of coolness which suggests she's coming at the topic from the direction of detach. "And have delivered the documents I need to lodge an insurance claim for my clinic. Arson, of course."

"Of course," Kian murmurs. "Well done."

There's a moment's pause, and then she says: "Kian."

Her tone is faintly exasperated, the sort where she knows there's something he's not saying, and frankly that's an achievement given how short a time they've known each other. It's delightful, really. Kian does not smile, however. "I don't believe that Carruthers is the one who burned down your clinic," he explains, almost apologetically, as he goes to lean against the back of the armchair nearest her, so they can speak without shouting across the room. "I asked him about it, and he reacted with righteous indignation at a time when he had no reason to lie."

She sits for some moments, watching him with brow furrowed. "Carruthers did not destroy my clinic," she murmurs, testing the words for herself, and then looking at him again. "Who did?"

"I don't know," Kian answers, "and I intend to find out."

She lifts an eyebrow, very delicately. "I would prefer to be reimbursed monetarily."

Kian laughs. "Quite so, quite so. You need to rebuild your clinic." He sobers. "In this case, consider it my civic duty; someone who would burn down a healer's clinic is a wildcard no one wishes to leave unidentified."

Ingram watches him for a moment and then nods, perfunctorily accepting. She rises with a piece of paper, mostly handwritten, and holds it out. "Then, my invoice."

Goodness; had she been working on this all night? Kian braces himself and takes it, and runs his eye down the list of charges. He does not show his wince; he had, after all, been expecting the hefty fees given what he'd put her through. "Ah," he murmurs, and turns to tap Connor's head lightly with the handle of his cane so the skeleton looks up. "This is relevant to you. For rental of the skeleton."

Connor looks from him to Ingram, examining her with green-lit eyes in a way that seems to be almost foreboding; and his shoulders lift in a blasé shrug, and he goes back to polishing.

"I suppose that means I'm not getting my skeleton back," Ingram murmurs, resigned.

"Au contraire, my dear healer." Kian gives her a quick smile. "You could hardly *not*. It's simply being returned to you with ... a little more than it had." She stares, and looks from him to the skeleton and back, and the look on her face is torn between intrigue and disbelieving antipathy. Kian can't help but laugh, and then bow, apologetically. "I do apologise for the additional unrequested. Unfortunately, there's little I can do about it. To send him back now would be tantamount to murder, even for a necromancer; and besides, for him to replace something he may have killed is far too inherent in his story to attempt to circumvent."

Cú Chulainn — Culann's hound, become so to replace a hound that the boy Sétanta had killed. The look on Ingram's face indicates her resigned understanding, but she sighs nevertheless, and folds her arms, and nods to the invoice. "Very well. I suppose this means I shall need to register my ownership of a reaver with the church?"

"I shall do so for you when I go to give them my medical expenses," Kian assures her cheerfully.

"Fine. Have you finished reading, yet?"

That seems rather pointed. Kian returns his attention to the invoice, running through them to the bottom, where the final item on the list is a reduction of the overall fee for the price of a good cup of coffee from the hotel's restaurant.

Kian laughs again, and this time there is nothing at all sarcastic in it; and he folds the invoice and bows toward Ingram. "Healer Ingram, I would be delighted to fulfil *all* items on this invoice."

Some of the tension escapes out of her shoulders, and she lifts her chin. "Good."

"I have but one question, however," Kian adds with his most charming smile, and she gives him a look that supposes it is frosty, and yet is more amused than not.

"Yes?"

"What, pray tell, *is* your first name?"

ALSO BY

Makari Clove & Pur Durance

Voice & Vein
(https://books2read.com/u/mgEN90)

Sunlight & Bone
(https://books2read.com/u/mgEN7v)

Blood & Nerve
(https://books2read.com/u/4EKELO)

Breath & Name
(https://books2read.com/u/bpaN8X)

ABOUT THE AUTHOR(S)

Makari co-authors Broadsides, and writes for video games under a separate name. She writes science fiction and fantasy for work and personal satisfaction, and finds the drive for creating keeps her hands busy in all spheres of life.

• • • • • • • • • •

Pur Durance is the co-author of Broadsides and the author of Base Seven, both contemporary fantasies of different flavours. Aurichalcum Publishing is her self-publishing vehicle (vroom vroom).

www.ingramcontent.com/pod-product-compliance
Lightning Source LLC
Chambersburg PA
CBHW050728180626
46814CB00002B/654